A DAY,
A NIGHT,
ANOTHER DAY,
SUMMER

A DAY,
A NIGHT,
ANOTHER DAY,
SUMMER

Christine Schutt

A HARVEST BOOK
HARCOURT, INC.
Orlando   Austin   New York
San Diego   Toronto   London

www.HarcourtBooks.com

Grateful acknowledgment is made to the following magazines, where these stories first appeared in slightly different form: *Alaska Quarterly Review, American Voice, Blackbird, Denver Quarterly, Kenyon Review, NOON, Shade, Unsaid,* and *Web del Sol.*

First published by TriQuarterly Books, Northwestern University Press, 2005

Library of Congress Cataloging-in-Publication Data
Schutt, Christine, 1948–
A day, a night, another day, summer/Christine Schutt.—1st Harvest ed.
p. cm.
"A Harvest Book."
First published: Evanston, Ill.: TriQuarterly Books/Northwestern University Press, 2005.
1. Abused women—Fiction. I. Title.
PS3569.C55555D39   2006
813'.54—dc22   2005030789
ISBN-13: 978-0-15-603066-3   ISBN-10: 0-15-603066-7

Text set in Garamond Premier

Printed in the United States of America

First Harvest edition 2006
A C E G I K J H F D B

for David

Contents

A DAY,
A NIGHT,
ANOTHER DAY,
SUMMER

DARKEST OF ALL

The years, she saw, fell heavily as books: the missing husband pinging a racket against the chuff of his hand, her charmed sister at the rental's beach, the raging Jean herself. In a coil of towel, the little boy named Jack was powdered free of sand. She tended to him then—absent, curious, easeful—and he calmed under the warmth of her hand. Now Jack's body was his own and not a thing she felt branched of, her hands growing out of; mother and son, they had even smelled the same once, when Jack's teeth were growing in. Now she did not get close enough—did not want to get close enough—to smell him. Jack's skin was given over to the wild fluctuations of his age, which meant it was one day clear and smooth, and the next erupted, and still later newly healed and probably sore. Now the boy smoked.

It was what he asked for first with the smoke of something smoked down clouding around his head: "Did you remember cigarettes?" Yes, yes, her soft assent. "But what I need," Jack said, "are socks." Snack foods, paper, stamps: the listlessly articulated list from every visit grew as the corridors grew, or so it seemed to Jean as she walked through the swabbed facility with its smell of Lysol and fish!

"Stamps," Jack said, "are what I really need. I want to write to friends."

Jack said, "I wrote myself here," and he showed Jean what he did every night on the edge of the table, which was a deeply scarred table, full of dates and initials, profanations, codes, and there on the edge, his knife-worked JACK. Jack said, "I want people to know I've been here and that I was okay. I had friends. Fuck," he said, "I've made a lot of friends," and so he had. An odd assortment said hello or made motions to speak to Jack each time they bumped past.

Jean said to Jack, "So what do you do with your friends?"

"They're not all friends," he said. "Some of them"—and he pointed to a boy with an old black face and voluptuously muscled body—"that guy," Jack said, "already has a kid. He's been in jail. And the fat girl bit a girl for trying to comb her hair. I don't talk to that crazy. Nobody does. There were stitches. That's how bad it was."

How bad it was Jean told her sister. Jean called the place the facility, eschewing its bucolic name and using Jack's slang when she was angry. Then she called the facility a dry-out place, a place for rehab on the cheap. A motel or a conference center, the facility had past lives in the same way as did its staff. First name only, confessing only their abuse, the pallid staff wore cushioned shoes and shuffled small steps. Their talk, too, was small and coughed out with erasures from whatever they saw looking back—not that, not that—but ahead, the home contract, the dickered pact, the rules to school the house against the wily abuser. "Addiction," the staff said, "we've been there—and been there. Relapse is common with friends still using." The staff twitched matches, frantically serene.

Jean told her sister, "These are the guys helping Jack with his homework. These are the people meant to be his friends."

But Jean's sister, being her sister, and wiser, Jean's sister said, "This is where Jack should be."

The hours at the facility were blocked and named: group, individual, free. "I'm climbing steps," Jack said, smiling. "I'm making progress here, Mother. You'd be proud!"

Jack. She was used to the shard of his name since he shortened it. His hair color, too, had changed, was leaden and beaten by the last school's cap, the same he wore through the meeting.

"Jack!" she said.

"What?" he asked.

Mother, son, counselor, here they were again, the weekend group in consultation: *family* was the name on the schedule.

Who was getting better? she wondered. Who was sick?

Jean asked her wiser sister, "Am I?"

"Are you?" she asked back.

Yes, it was all too common a story—Jean knew, she admitted as much—a woman on her own and what she had to do because of the children. Because of them she had to ask the missing husband for what he did not have that yet was needed.

"Look at what I've had to do for money," Jean said, home again, on the couch with the quiet son, Ned. The men she had let wander into the apartment. Think of them! And she did—and didn't he? "Don't you think of them sometimes?"

Ned said, "I was very young, Mother."

It was Jack, years older, who had said he remembered a man who shook her upside down for quarters.

"Oh," Jean moaned as Ned was getting to and scratching some unreachable places. "Oh, I hope you don't remember," she said. Then, "Yes! That feels good!" she said, and said again, "That feels good!" and Jean let her towel drop in a way that made her wonder since there wasn't a man to put lotion on her back should she ask her son to do it.

Jean, at the facility, said to the counselor, "Ask Jack what he did with my bank card. I bet he didn't tell you." Freely

spending with the purpose to be caught, it seemed, Jack
had bought what in the moment moved him, leaving waxy,
bunched receipts between the sheets for her to find of
what he had signed for with abandon, largely. Felonious
boy, that Jack! Skulking the facility, as she had seen him,
butting what he passed—doors, walls, wheeled racks hung
with visiting coats—Jack scared Jean a little, and she came
home tired.

And Ned was tired! Tired from scratching. Tired from the
yawn of Saturday, from homework, from art class, from
girls. From streets and apartments, cigarettes, beers—from
more girls. On almost any Sunday, late in the morning and
cragged in a gray sheet, the boy slept in his room, which
was also gray. Thin light, lingering smoke. Something there
was about Ned gray, too: the pale skin of his outstretched
leg, blue-black hair in a cuff at his ankle. Only his foot, the
heel of it, was full of color—not old pavement to be ra-
zored—Ned's foot was young. It invited petting, touching
to say, Wake up. "Wake up," she said, looking at the covered boy because she did not want to see what was on the
bedside table, although Jean saw it clearly: the cigarettes
first, the ashy spill around the glasses, orange juice pips on
the rim of the old-fashioned. Haywire spirals yanked out
of notebooks, Post-its curling on the tops of papers: *See
me!* one of them said. Jean was looking at the screen-dead

computer. The drawers, too, she saw but did not open. She knew enough about Ned. She knew he drank and smoked, carried condoms, broken jewelry. She knew he liked to kiss; he liked the girls. Girls, girls, girls, girls. Their voices ribboned out from faces closely pressed against the cradle of the phone—babies still, most often shy. "Is Ned there?" they asked.

"I'm sorry," Jean said—and said—"he's still asleep."

Lifted in the wind, the blinds banged their music on the sill; it was a sound of diminutive breakage—of saucers, of cups—in a rhythm like the rising and falling of a chest, like breathing, a boy's, his. Tiptoed and unsteady, she silenced the phone next to his bed. She put the ringer on off—and why not? The callers for Ned would call back, so let him sleep, she thought, another hour. Let him grow in his twisted sheets! Bent, crooked, an impression of bones he was, a tent of bones, a sudden arm slung above his head and the black tuft of hair there as startling as his sex.

Think of something else, think of the Sunday papers. Consider this fall's color on girls stood back-to-back, with their skinny arms crossed, as girls crossed them, coyly. The girls who visited Ned stood at the door coyly, toed in and stooped with baby backpacks on their backs, asking from behind ragged bangs, "Is Ned home?"

"Yes," she had to say, "but still asleep."

And Jack? Jack was now so tipped against the sun—the bright shard of his name again—that just to speak of Jack hurt Jean's eyes; and she did not want to think about the place where she had been or what Jack was doing there or what he would be doing there at night in the facility.

"Not knowing where he sleeps is fine by me," Jean admitted, but only to Ned. To Ned she complained. Now when she sat on the couch, still red from washing off the facility, she said, "Jack makes me believe he has paid for whatever it is we are doing to him. Does that make sense?" She said, "Please, my back."

Ned said, "You never made Jack do this."

Sometimes Ned used a comb on her back. He made tracks and designs with the comb. He wrote his name and asked, "So what did I write then?"

She sat on the couch, tickled by the comb tracking through the lotion, and she said to Ned, "I can't help my-self sometimes. When I am in family I say terrible things...." And she told the boy what things she had said about a man who was yet the father—and she knew that, yet she would speak. She wanted to tell Ned everything. Now, every weekend, it seemed, she came home parched and queasy, calling out to Ned, "Are you here? Anybody home? Yes? No? Who else?"

Once a girl with rainbow hair lay unbuttoned on Ned's bed. The girl was quick to sit up, and she smiled at Jean,

distraction of the girl's hair, knotted and skyward
however the girl had been with him, was such that
saw was the girl's hair and those parts erect from
tugging. Just look at the girl's stubby nipples! So this was
Ned's idea of pretty, Jean thought, and wondered, Was the
girl disappointed in her? Was she drab to the girl? For that
was how she felt.

"Is this your mother?" from the girl in a girl's voice, just
a whisper.

"Yes."

This was the mother breaking open gelcaps and licking up
sleep or the opposite of sleep, extreme wakefulness, speed.
This was the mother using scissors between her legs, staying ready, staying hairless, should someone want to lick
her.

Something Jean could never bring up at the family consultation in the facility was what she was doing at home
because she was hardly ever sober herself, but she was
prudent in her daily use of substances. She measured, she
counted, she observed fastidious rituals. She soaped and
creamed and powdered when the high was at her throat. At
night she drank—then only ales, wines, rarely hard liquor.
But she drank to ease the restlessness from the petty drugs
she took, gouging tinbacks with a pencil to release sealed

tablets, over-the-counter nondrowsy—four, six, eight pills a pop—uninspired habit, nothing serious, but growing, at the worst growing, at the worst becoming what her father's habit was: Vicodin, Prozac, Valium, Glucotrol, Synthroid, Mevacor, plain old aspirin. Jean's father had offered, saying, "I don't know what it's called, but it's good." No, no, no, Jean had resisted. She wanted most of her habit non-prescription and cheap.

No one noticed what she did.

This was especially true at the facility, where Jean had expected to be found out as if passing by a screen and seen clear through; but she slipped past and into the facility with her son and her son's counselor, and she was fearless again. Everyone was looking at Jack, asking him, "So what do you do around users?"

Jack said, "I don't."

Everyone agreed his was a good answer, clever.

Avoid some mothers, Jean thought, avoid me; the thought of being worse than the mother she remembered as having was hurtful, but not so hurtful as to keep her from using more expensive substances. The guilt didn't keep her from calling Suzette and speaking in their code, "I need some panty hose," and welcoming the girl at any time of the night—even introducing Suzette to Ned. "We work together," she had said. A traveling house of a girl come to them at any hour, a bulk, a shape zippered or buckled, pilot glasses, sneakers, Peruvian hat, Suzette didn't much surprise Ned. He was used to interruption, to the phone at odd hours and hand-delivered gifts, the rustle of things dried, split pods, seeds flying. The flare-up affairs with names Jean might use for weeks—Nora, Mark, David, Marlene—Ned was familiar with this much of the life his mother had in another part of the city.

The city, if only that were to blame, but there was her own father, the one who managed to be sick in the country. Jean's father couldn't remember Jean's address or the names of the boys, saying, "Your oldest will be sixteen before I see him," when Jack was almost eighteen yet already sick the way he was. And Jean was sick, too—and maybe Ned. The baby creases of his neck often smelled of smoke, greasy exudations from the bonfired night, tin bright, pin size, salty.

"Oh, God," Jean said, and Jean's careful sister asked—and asked often—if Jean was taking anything she shouldn't.

Jean said, "Nothing. Why should I?"

Once Jean let Ned visit Jack, and she was happy to have Ned's company, and Jack was made happy, too, just to see his brother. They shivered to be near before they touched and were teasing again, boys again, brothers. The brothers walked together and apart from Jean, waving at their mother with their smoking hands because they could, being here, at the facility. Look at the troughs of sand used for ashtrays! They were mad smokers here at the facility, but what else was there to do, Jack asked, except to smoke and answer questions and earn steps? Every week he reached a new level; now there was talk about a contract.

"The home contract is something we agree on," Jack said, "if I'm to come back to the city and live with you."

He showed Jean a draft. To the question about curfew, he had written, *None*.

Jack said, "Shit, Mother, I snuck out all the time."

"So where were you going?" Jean asked; but when he made to speak, she said, "Don't tell me."

She didn't want to read Jack's home contract either and not, as it happened, when Ned was along and all of them sitting at the gashed table with Jack pointing. "See? My name's all over this fucking place."

"Jack, please!" Jean said.

"I've lived without a curfew," Jack said, and every weekend said, "I've changed. I'm on the third step. I want my medal."

At the scarred table with her sons, Jean cried. "There is so much to be sorry about," she said, but her sons were embarrassed, it seemed to her, and sad and scornful of her rustling for a hankie. "Anyone?" she asked. "I'm sorry." She bent her head, snuffling, using a cloth when she found one. "I'm sorry," she said. "I'll be all right."

The story Jean most often told Ned was about Jack and what Jack did. She told Ned of the friends his brother had made at the facility, even the fat girl now, the one who had bitten a girl for approaching with a comb, even she was his friend. Jack said he was popular, the most popular kid. Jean said, "I think he thinks he is running for class president." Jean said, "Where does he think he is?"

In family, Jack said he wanted to live in L.A. He said he was old enough, he had worked last summer, he had had the responsibility of a job.

"Putting up boxes!" Jean said.

Jack said to the counselor, "Do you understand now? Do you see what I've been saying? Look at her!"

Jean, in passing Ned's room, said, "I don't want to talk about your brother."

Ned said, "Mother!" Sometimes he said, "It's not your fault," and he offered, "I'll rub your back if you'll rub mine." Sometimes he said, "Why do you listen to Jack?"

Ned said, "I don't know. I don't know the answers to all your questions."

Ned said, "Why should I?" when the question of curfews came up. "Jack didn't."

Sometimes Ned got angry and his hand, long still against her back, withdrew, and he went to his room and turned up his music. The telephone rang; he slammed the door or he talked to Jean in the way his brother did, absently: the flat-voiced "Yes," the "What?" that was nasty. The nimble imitative skill Ned showed was common. Jack did it and others of his friends and Ned's friends, she had heard them speaking to their parents in their parents' voices. They groaned new words that meant dumb and ugly. She said, "Talk to me in your own voice, Ned, talk to me so I can understand."

Sometimes Ned did speak earnestly, and when he spoke to her in this voice, she wanted to take him by surprise, to touch him, to kiss his mouth as it moved—and would go on moving, saying, "Mother! Don't!"

Sometimes Ned said, "Will you not, please," but she went on. She wormed her fingers between his toes; she tickled him or worked Q-tips, painfully, around the curled folds of his ears. "Damn it, Mother, that hurts!" Yet he was the one who asked her to do it. "Cut my nails," Ned said, and she cut too close.

She said and she said and she heard herself saying—whining, really—"Please, you are the only one who knows how to scratch."

Hadn't she heard? Jack asked; but, no, the sound of a body thrown against a wall was not a sound she had ever heard. The sound of a hand raised against another body, yes, that was familiar to her, and objects ripped, broken, smashed, whipped, snapped, yes; wails against a scurrilous tirade she had heard many times before, and the blast of her own voice was familiar. Think of all that noise! So what did Jack know compared to her?

"Plenty," Jack said, and he read from his home contract delirious stories. What he had done and what in the future, once home again, he would contract not to do: no more drugs with lyrical names; those suggestive tabs of magic, he vowed he would not take—no, not again, never again. He didn't need to be high. He was going to think.

Meetings, yes, he agreed to go to them, to find them.

Strategies for avoiding users: avoid users.

Curfew.

Curfew was always an issue.

Every weekend Jean repeated, "Write it down! No later than one o'clock!" when Jack, of course—of course, extreme!—said, he said, "The home contract has to do with trust. No."

Then she thought of Jack as he appeared in his home contract stories, the ones he wrote so freely, attaching pages to the contract, pulling from his pocket more stories penciled on folded notes with linty seams and so worn in their appearance that she wondered: Had Jack started these stories before the facility? Was he writing these scary stories while they were happening at home to Jack, the school actor—always dramatic?

The starless urban nights he described, kiosks on corners, the shuddering homeless, Jack and his buddies, whoever at the time, even he didn't always remember which friends but that there were several, and they walked the city. They stood in the sheeted stalls on busy streets—all-night markets in awful light; but the surly cashiers sold them anything: imported beers and cigarettes, for which they pooled their money. Jack had stolen from his mother to buy what he snorted in bathroom stalls. He stole so largely he was caught.

"Look at the pages I've got!" he said and thumbed the home contract.

Home, in a tub she kept hot, she sweat out the smell of the scrub used at the facility; she soaped; she flexed her toes and admired the polish she still put on, insisting she would yet be playful, as once she had been playful, surely, and perverse and curious and young. On her knees, in a bathroom, she hung over the tub and watched, as he did, a small rising.

Oh, they had their casual routine. Jean and Ned, the

two of them, she thought, living well together and easily, passing even shyly in the hall, sliding against the wall to keep from touching. Observant, quiet, gently agreeing or asking on the way out, "Do you want anything?" This was the way they were together, alone, Jack at the facility and the husband years missing.

Tub-pink and powdered, holding out the lotion, asking, "Will you do my back now, please?" Often asking, "Please, my back?"

"Please, stay home," she called out, but Ned did less and less. And less and less he called, or when he did his voice was muzzy, or else he sounded angry and baffled. "What's the number where you are?" Jean asked and heard him speak to someone near, "Whose house is this? Where are we?"

Oh! To have those summers back and time on the rental's beach, a weathered house where sand collected on the windowsills and grass blades thatched the mudroom. Country on a small green scale was what she told her sister that she missed. Jean missed the sloppy blossoms that were roses, beach roses, casual pink daubs against the fence and sugared sand. Blown before picked, the beach roses, perfuming the air as a girl would, largely indiscriminate, the beach roses Jean missed and the smell of them and the colors of this country, which was not the country she drove through on her way to the facility. No, that country—why talk of it?

Jack only talked about the city, about his enemies and friends. Cale, Urbinger, Schwartz were guys out to get him when Jack got back, which was one of the reasons he feared going back and joked of never leaving the facility. Fucking Urbinger claimed Jack had stolen his watch and that he, Jack, owed him.

"Jack," Jean said.

"What?" Jack asked. "What is it?"

The tabs he let melt on his tongue were easy to come by in the parks where he dangled in the stories he was telling—dopey sleeper—waking to the skaters' whir, the poor's hobbled passing. Gnawed-at gnawing rats, bald and balding, tamed up his leg snooting food—that's how still Jack was, watching: island drummers, bobbers in exploded shoes, the man in his python, parading his snake. Venomous keepers, women padlocked—threaded lips, encrusted ears—the faces Jack saw had the caught look of fish. Fishy, guilty, up to no good, they were passing out cards to any hand that would take one, and he did, didn't he? "So much in the city is easy to come by," Jack said, which was what he was about. The story was his; some of it was attached to the home contract. "The Z-B Club," Jack said, "is real. It happens near the park every night."

The friends Jack described jingled in Jean's ears when she

listened to Jack's story. The braid beads on girls, the strung shells, buttons, bells they wore around their necks, several at a time—yoked, choked—the sounds they made, the chafe of jeans when they walked, the chafe of candy-colored lighters: sweet cannabis smoke! The club lights expose the air confettied with drugs, with curlicues of edible, mind-bending paper. That stupid Cale got sick—and almost died—but he was rushed to Lenox Hill. "Where I live," Jack said, "is dangerous. That's why I need the home contract. I need some rules to live by."

Jean came home from the facility and soaked in hot water until she was warm again and asked Ned to please put some lotion on her back. "I don't care if it is cold," she said. She wore her bathrobe as a stole, shrugging to where she wanted it. "There," Jean said, "and there."

In the gourd-green and -yellow of October, on sullen afternoons, Jean watched Jack carve JACK along the rim of the mutilated table in the dining hall. He was putting his own name everywhere, chipping at it while he lured his mute friends with smut. Boys with home-done haircuts and scars, they touched themselves lightly and laughed. She had walked toward this same scene before and seen them and seen Jack, slunk in his stories—then, then, then—gouging the table with a fork.

Jean was afraid for Jack. Jack was such a baby! Jean was afraid for him when she looked to where he slept in the cinder block facility: two floors, picture windows. B movies, fifties sets, people sashed in bloody curtains were what Jean saw looking up to where Jack lived. The facility had once been something else—a health club, a retreat, a motel? There was the empty swimming pool just beyond the patio—another good spot for a death. Here were crazies who would bite a hand that moved to touch them. And such sounds Jean had heard, lonesome and wild, streaking past Jack when he was on the phone to her and cowled, as she imagined, secretive, shoving off others, saying, "Asshole! I'm talking to my mother!"

"Who is it?" Jean asked.

"No one," he said. "This kid."

The sky cleared; the horizon was precise. She asked Ned, "What do you think about Jack? What did you think about what he said? Did you believe him?" Jean asked, "Can someone mix all those drugs and stand?" She asked, "Do you think Jack's any better?"

Ned said, "How should I know? I wasn't there."

Home from the beach! The little boys come home! The hair on their heads—matted shocks stuck up in sleep— was warmly fragrant of weeds and sea. Jean had liked to smell the boys. She had bent to their heads and sniffed, but their shirts! Always their shirts smelled worn and un-washed to her—sour, brown.

The beach in noon light was hurtful as foil to look at, and she didn't.

The beach in any light. In the white folds of Ned's skin, in the white folds of Jack's, she had fingered baby sweat. Jean had lifted the wisps of hair from off their baby scalps, marked as the moon, with their stitched plates of bone yet visible, the boys; how often she had thought to break them.

YOUNG

Sometimes I surprised myself and went to where my young husband was sitting—and he was often sitting, inky, cross, a writing tablet under his arm—and I went down on my knees. I was between his legs on the night I first met her, the girl of this story; and again when the doorbell rang and rang with our neighbor on the care of the shared garden, I was in his lap.

"Human hair balled in nylons keeps the deer away. Beetles eat the roses, but in this climate everything grows," our neighbor said.

Molds, I thought of, all kinds of fungus.

Nothing bad had ever happened to me; my father was sending us money, and my young husband and I were grateful. I wrote thank-you notes on heavy cards vined with my initials. I had a new last name and told my young husband, and anyone who asked, that I liked it. I said I had always wanted to be at the end of the alphabet, and this was true, but I was lying when I said I wanted to meet new people. My fantasy was to be crippled enough to be allowed to read in bed all day, yet when I wanted to go to the theater, I could. I bought tickets to a lot of plays and lied about the cost. I lied about money. Sometimes we had less and sometimes more than I reported. But who would have known what cut flowers cost? The tulips were expensive! Common, yes, ordinary, nothing of the wistful about them, nothing poetical, but they were clean and sturdy, and I went on lying about how much flowers cost. I lied about other things, too, sometimes fantastically, even garishly. Any story about where the girl and I went was untruth; I embellished.

Amsterdam for the weekend—not likely!

And what was expected of me?

We were visitors, my young husband and I, and we were ignorant. Should we consider the garden beds our business, too? we wondered. And could we cut the roses, or were we just to mow the grass? Other concerns I had were over dates, rivers, architectural styles; I wanted to know. What was a caryatid, an obelisk, a cataract? I had to look up new words and many of the same words. *Pusillanimous* was one I could never remember! The girl taught me how to say *Magdalen* on a day full of histories—this is where and this is where and this is where it happened. Here indeed was an English friend when the brusque wind that was our neighbor smelled of garden. "I am used to," our neighbor whined on and on, "I am used to." Water, rake, prune. That garden was all of the time.

Eventually we fought over it, the neighbor and I, but the garden came with the flat as shared. It was shared, yet I was too shy to walk freely in it, and my young husband had other tours in mind.

Alone, arrived at the British Museum, I walked toward the great sooty columns and into the shadowed interior; skirts, I heard, and whisperers scuffling past. Heroines, full of restraint, circled medieval weaponry: Fanny Price and Lucy Snow, commonly known—like the tulips—yet I favored them as heroines. They had integrity, and though I did not, I strove to be better and was inspired by my visits to the manuscript rooms. Seals, documents, signatures— their makers really lived!

I tramped along the Long Water alone, and sometimes my young husband came, too, but what I wanted was a dog. I had some breeds in mind, and we went to kennel shows to see them. We pretended we were buying, or I pretended, and my young husband indulged me. He let me stay to see the setters show off in the ring. He let me coo and calculate the cost. Much too much money!

This is the woman I was then, spoiled, fearful, idolatrous, a mix that our neighbor, I think, recognized. A big box in a car coat, our neighbor stood at the gate to the garden, and I stood at the window looking down at her. We looked at each other for what felt like a long time, unsmiling and curious, seeming to ask, What is it like where you live?

I missed home and I didn't miss home. I said I could live here forever just to be surrounded by the scribbling ghosts. My young husband was scribbling something. Situated, alert, he quoted E. P. Thompson from *The Making of the English Working Class*. I quoted some writers, too, a bit more obvious, yes, but love poems: "Now thou hast lov'd me one whole day, To morrow when thou leav'st, what wilt thou say?" We took ourselves seriously. We were foolish, but we believed—or I did—that in another country we might take up our work; here, in a place where every third house had its plaque, its honored dead, we might see what we were meant to do, and we might know to do it.

It was all this not knowing. What are you going to do and what are you going to do? At least here were no nearby parents to ask, "What happens now?" We were living far away in a watery country; brush past the shrubbery and it spilled. I loved it, England, yes. Mostly I wanted to be here and not home. The rock walls greened in the fissures, and the terraces were overgrown—woodbine, musk rose, eglantine. Shakespeare's benevolent spirit. Keats once, alone along Well Walk; but the dead in the galleries were women who had suffered in love—as who had not?—only these women were famous for it. Say anything, teach anything, prove anything, monsieur; I can listen now.

❧

I did not always want to listen to my young husband speak. His voice, I thought, was flat and had no music—and neither did mine, which was reason enough to be quiet. On buses, in taxis, I often put my finger to my lips. After the theater, with the accents in our ears, it was best to be quiet.

The rain made us quiet and kept us indoors with books, and I was happy. I liked reading, and I still liked bringing my young husband off in the fogged winter light. It seemed then that our bodies were English pale and that the rain against the window made rivulets of shadow—did it? Was the night sky I saw quite so pink?

I wasn't sure.

I wasn't sure of a lot of things after they had happened.

A new morning, January, Magdalen, the deer park, I was without my young husband and in the girl's company. The frozen grass was still green, very hard underfoot. My shoes were flimsy and wet, while the girl, I saw, was wearing boots—Wellingtons, of course, why not?

Or else she wore high heels with leather pants.

Other sounds, sighing.

Her everyday shoes swiped like rags against the floor; her lips stuck when she licked them to talk. I licked them for her—ah!

Too fast.

First came the cashmere sweater with its voluptuous neck, then the tapered houndstooth slacks, the wrist-thin ankles, the narrow foot. These parts of her belonged to a girl from a glamorous home and endless funds to live by. Sidesaddle in the chair, she was wearing rolled against her neck this luscious red sweater. She was fair; she was slight. Oh, she was and she was! The tangles she thumbed off her comb I took up on an impulse that surprised me. The way I had always felt about shed hair in lockets or worked into bracelets and clasped was that shed was dirty.

But I took up strands of her, took up her lipstick, the fringe she wore for underwear. "May I?" I asked and borrowed belts with buckles from another century to be bound up with her, a tartan girl in mist and lamplight, a girl in a winter coat the rain had beaded.

We stayed too long in the bedsit.

The bedsit was hers, a place tunneled to through dank cobbled streets the color of slime. The journey was cold, but the bedsit was very warm. I put my leg near the source and felt burned, yet hours and hours went by in her bedsit, and we were late for what was planned.

My young husband asked, "Is the bedsit her idea of poor?" He also said, "Go! Get out! It will do you good!" So I went to the theater when what he meant for me was join the wives, those Bermondsey mavens after trivets and toast racks, fish knives and forks. "Ivory soaked in milk gets the stains out," I learned, and I learned about churches. So, so that was the apse, that the transept, the aisle. The wives of young husbands I met had, many of them, taken up stone rubbing. On their knees and in their overcoats, they rubbed as under tents. I thought they looked like lily pads. The floors they knelt on, and I knelt on with them, the floors were pond colored, uneven, cold. Our coats were no protection. The girl had me over to get warm. She stood close; her close breath smelled of tea. Slight breasts, hip bones, lips. Then I was on my knees again, on my stone-rubbing knees, and my knees were sore. The harsh carpet hurt.

I tend to rush.

The night she leaned over to kiss my hand, my hand held out on the table, that time the candles singed my hair, that time we leaned so close was it beekeeping or Quentin Bell—what were we talking about when I said, "Me, too, yes"? I said, "Yes, the same way, me, too," and later I tried to write it out to her, and what I said was corny but stupidly, stupidly true!

The girl was, was . . . I was word poor, tongue tied, half-way embarrassed, but why, in the first place, did I write to her? The letter was smeared in the rain when I mailed it—but I mailed it.

"Why did you?" was what my young husband asked, but this was later.

Another time my young husband was with us and sat on the floor of her bedsit in his coat. He had been away.

I believed my young husband. He could have! I believed him when he said he had been in the States staying with his parents, asking for money and more time abroad, giving excuses, showing the notes for a book. I believed he had a book although I had not seen it.

And never, never did I think that he was lying, that he was, as I was, making calls to someone, saying, "I meant to, but I didn't," saying, "I'm afraid," saying, "Where?"

Except that I was young, why did so much of what happened surprise me?

I did not want to be married. That was the feeling I had when I opened the closet door and saw his side of things, which was so much like my side of things, rumpled and slung, that I thought we were unsafe, and I was afraid.

We were too much alone.

We were too much alone with no reason to wake and slept on and on with even the curtains open. Nothing could wake us. We slept on, then stayed up late with weekend visitors, mostly unexpected yet all related. They came

with traveler's checks and maps, saying tricky words aloud
because, I think, like me they were proud of knowing how
Leicester, Glyndebourne, St. John were pronounced. And
the names themselves, the English had such names! Per-
severing oaks of names, deeply stained copper beaches. I
wondered why had I picked his name, my young husband's
last name. What did I hope to do with a name no one
could pronounce?

The girl—oh, to be as smart as that! Pouncing lightly on
Virginia Woolf the way she did, saying, "The books are all
chorus and no plot." Who cared if the ideas were not always original? The girl was professorial and sure; complex
sentences expressed complex thoughts. Pater and Ruskin.
Caryatid, I knew she would know it.

Other excitements.

The way she drank leaving some of what she drank on
her lips.

"Kiss me."

"Here?"

"Kiss me!"

The slipknot of laughter was so easily loosed in her.

"Be an adult," she said, "be false and effusive," and I
was. When my young husband came through the door, I
jumped off the bed and kissed him, too. I told him how
glad I was to see him back.

"Just in time to help me with the garden," I said, but we did nothing to the garden. The shared garden was bearded by July, and our neighbor complained. First on the phone, then in person, she asked, "Are you making a meadow?" Her notes hissed under the door. Two, three, four of them, none were answered—how could I? The very way she wrote, her backward-slanting, pinched characters looked more like ants to me than letters, ants marching over creamy paper. *You, you, you, you, you.*

At night the ditch in the middle of the bed, the numbers illumined on the clock. I felt movement when, back-to-back, I tried to sleep with him. He had bad dreams and woke up moaning and lay as in a coffin, wide awake. My young husband was thinking about his future. He said he was thinking about business school, which took me by surprise. He was thinking about making money—and he did! Or so I am told. The friends who still see him say.

We were young.

At a pub once and under swags of weeds we were meant to kiss by, my young husband said I was a fool.

What could we have been talking about when he said, "You don't know a thing about me"? He said, "You never did." *But I thought, I thought, I thought* was the way a lot of my sentences started then with him, then with her. Youth and appetite! Something else about this part of my life, when I spent most nights with a man I called my young husband—I kicked him for not coming sooner to the rescue with the cigarettes. I called him names at restaurants when I was drunk with visitors. I said, "Who knows?" when anyone asked me what he was doing. I said he was a liar when I was a liar, too. I went out of my way to hurt him, spending too much money—I was mean to my young husband, and I often no more knew why that was than I knew what it had to do with our lives.

And there was more that was significant. Her teeth, her lips, her lip-like part. And more, more you should know, how, about to board the plane for home, my young husband broke the bottle of expensive wine that he had saved so conspicuously. The wine was red, of course, and ran under and around my shoes.

DO YOU THINK I AM WHO I WILL BE?

He bought a lunch that needs water to make, and he took a long and sour piss. The fan is broken; he feels sick. The lilies he was sent last week look afflicted; the petals, scummy. After only a short fragrance, the lilies are wrinkling to a faded dirty pink; but he cannot give them fresh water, and in the moment he hates where he lives. Glass spikes the walls that separate the back lots' tired gardens: brick borders, wilted impatiens. No one is home to water.

Water again. He would feel a whole lot better if he could stand in a shower and think, but there's the water again. Water is part of his problem. NO WATER WEDNES-DAY—the sign has been up for days in the elevator. How could he forget except that he forgets? Explanations, probabilities. Who is it on the phone he does not answer and when he does hangs up? "Who is this?" he asks, thinking, Madeline!—but he hears only fuzz. The clock, too, is doing something.

He has known Madeline from when she was a smaller version of what she is now.

Is it five o'clock already? He cannot distinguish sounds with so much screaming around him.

Children and animals.

Somewhere in the apartment is a dog, or else the stained impress on the throw rug is a shadow. He can't smell dog, but there are signs. The worn paint along the doorjamb from where the dog abased himself and the fact of too much dust point to dog. Dog and the city! It is noisy and dirty just as they said.

They, they, the folks back home (his mother, really), he still thinks he can call her, and he picks up the phone for the fun . . . and Jesus Christ! Wouldn't you know it! Over the noise he can hear a far-off voice. He treats the phone as if he has been listening in, and he hangs up carefully. He didn't come home to talk to anybody except, perhaps, Madeline. He would make an exception for Madeline, especially. She writes, *I will write him a letter, but I can't excuse myself.* She writes that she has met another David, this time named Ralph. Silly name, really, unless it rhymes with *chafe,* the way the English say it. "Rafe, strafe, abrade, grate, rake," he speaks aloud to himself, and adds *scour* and *blister* to the list. *Here is okay,* she writes, *actually, I think here is good.*

Flayed is the last word he thinks of when he reads how she hopes they can meet sometime. *We should although ???when???* Her visible evasions, the fence of question marks she puts around *when*—these gestures hurt his feelings; but after a drink, it won't bother him at all, the unlikeliness of their meeting.

Their unlikeliness.

Love of this kind has flared before in him; he has been pursued and has, himself, pursued. Madeline, especially. Dear Madeline.

His desk is in the light he left on from this morning.

This morning he did not walk a dog although there is something doggy about his apartment; this room, hard lived here. Too much trash! And too many books he hasn't read. Their rightful owners must come back. If he puts his ear to the floor, and he puts his ear to the floor, he can hear slippers slapping toward him. He waits. He waits on his knees. He waits until the quiet, long unnoticed, disconcerts him. What is he supposed to do?

He walks through rooms and hears a woman's voice asking him, "What is it you want?" Most of what he knows comes from putting his face up close. The resinous dope box he sniffs at now is for how he used to smell. He doesn't smoke anymore, but he drinks. He still drinks and he mixes with ice so the no-water Wednesday won't affect him. There are cubes left surely. No? No.

"*No* starts your every sentence," his old girlfriend said, or else she said, "Don't!"

Fuck her! Now that he has his drink—without ice—and the light is still on at his desk, he can start. He is looking for a way to start, and he gets up from his desk to find it.

Dear Madeline.

The word he wants is *fouled.*

Who would have guessed? September, the sensible yet willing month, and suddenly so hot! He looks backward to when he last saw Madeline. Not in September, August, July, but, yes, in June, with the chestnut trees in their short-lived show, deeply green and bobbing—that's when he last saw her. That's when he last saw his old girlfriend, too. He saw the wells beneath her eyes, dark and wet from fucking. She was almost pretty, but when she stood, it was too much skin even for him; and it seems more terrible now when he thinks of Madeline.

Now, and what time is it now? The church hasn't bonged.

A cloud watcher, Madeline has said she is in love with light. Summer solstice is a grief she looks forward to, simultaneously loving the light and bemoaning that the light marks the beginning of days nightly shorn.

And now it is official, Madeline has written, *the start of the school year, and I am twenty-one!*

Nineteen ninety-five, 1996, 1997, 1998. To be all those years in Madeline's company and yet spared her anguish— *You're never really over it,* Madeline's words. He has been spared what has happened at home and what goes on happening, or so she says. "I admit it. I am bad, and I know my poor parents suffer!" Madeline in her high, protestant voice. "I can't help myself. I'm young." The ongoing moodiness that has sent her on record-time drives. Philadelphia to New York to Boston, New York to Vermont, Connecticut to New York, he has only heard about the trips, those midnight visits she makes so that she might sleep away from home.

In July was it? Madeline arrived at his place in expensive shoes—just straps—and a skirt the size of a dish towel. Mostly he had seen her in uniform. Year after year, lovelier. Glasses, contacts; braces, a mouth.

Midsentence, midsummer, they went outdoors and sat in the park, and Madeline yanked back her hair while speaking, tightly tied it, although it came undone. Again and again, she pulled back her hair, and he liked how she did this suddenly, expertly, fast, exposing a swimmer's face in its just-surfaced smoothness.

"My story is nothing special," she said then. "He likes that I'm a girl."

The arms she clasped around her legs are thin. She has no breasts to speak of, and the clothes she wears are throwaway thrift shop. Madeline has an orphan appeal, and her famished prettiness gives off heat.

The room is too warm. He says, "Some air in this stink box I live in will help," when he knows of no remedy.

Another time Madeline simply called to say that she was in town for an interview with a magazine or a TV station, something glamorous that had happened to her just because she is special.

꧁

Do you think I am who I will be? she writes with the prospect of graduation and the glamorous job. Half of him loves her and half hopes she fails.

His responses to her are always the same: *Great news, Good luck, Hope I see you.* He imagines her reading his letters. He imagines she yawns. He is not original, handsome, or young. Years are passing. Soon there will be snow underfoot by noon turned to slush. A wavy salt stain will abstract his shoes. Ice then, and weather soon. Her words in the park were "Mr. Gates"—laughing at him—"I will write you, Mr. Gates. I will e-mail! I will phone!"

Do you think I am who I will be? has years and years of future in it. How long has it been since he has seen her? Was it really last June, or the summer before, or even another year? There is joy to be had in what he is doing, teaching, but he has maxed out all his credit cards and lost sight of the joy and feels fucked. Glutted with the hoopla of passage and doughy skies and cold lawns—and the stupid napkins he has balled in his pocket!—toothpicks and addresses, presents and promises never to forget when he would like to forget, when he will forget and travel! Yes, he should go to Tibet for the cause. He should visit Prague fully funded. He should make more money, he should take time off, he should, he should, he should, he is thinking, shaking through the drawer for a coaster. He finds the dog collar in the same drawer, and he knows now with certainty where the smell comes from and why the cushions on the sofa are damp seeming, oily. He empties his pockets of the party and carries the collar around his room and into the kitchen again and back to his room again with a little more whiskey and a splash—there *is* water!—in a heavy glass. The heavy, cut-crystal glass, another clue, was left behind from when the dog lived here. He is almost certain that when the dog lived here, there was more to drinking; there was company on the couch. A lot of days felt like Saturday. It didn't matter if it rained, and even when she stopped kissing him, he didn't mind. He thinks of his old girlfriend demanding, "What is it you want?" Some days he knows. Today he wants whiskey, he wants to take off his party clothes, he wants to sleep on the couch. He wants no more faces—not even Madeline's.

He has caught his school cold, or else he is allergic, but to what? He can only think it is the dog who lived here and wonder how much of the dog is left. A collar, some rubbed-away places, but maybe there is hair? The old girlfriend's hair, he remembers, there wasn't very much of it. His own hair, too, is no more than smoke. The parched season is dangerous, and those who are sent to put out the fires thrash past in flames on the news. He is thirsty again, but he will not move. He sits at his desk and takes small breaths while the ravening dog scratches toward him.

WEATHER IS HERE,
WISH YOU WERE BEAUTIFUL

Whatever they saw looked vaguely obscene until their hearts kicked in. Then they were in a car going at easy speed past once-in-a-life fields full of a dawn and a beauty unexpected in the home state with the ugly name.

She did not like to say it.

So they passed a field of alfalfa, a field of corn, a border of trees. The red-and-white barns were all there was of people; even the animals, it seemed, were put away; only tuneless crows in heavy flight surprised them—and the sound of their own voices.

"What don't you want to tell me? Tell me what," she was shouting at the others—George mostly. The village scale on which she had lived was a greenhouse of sharp smells, and she was not worldly. She did not know, and she did not know unless George, sleeping near her, explained. George, in his nimbus of genius rumors, was a loose mouth asleep against her book bag, a loose, large, wet-looking mouth— too alive!—she had never kissed it. She wanted to be quits of that history of stains, no more the fishy smells on her sheets.

"I'm coming down," she said. "The high is passing through me."

Now she was sleepy and slightly depressed.

Oh, what was she doing in this car with these people?

Sam, the braggart, was smoking on the stoop and toting up what parts of him still worked. He was smoking and eating at the same time. He was smoking and eating and laughing at himself. They watched him squish soft fruit between his teeth.

Other annoyances, hers, Sam on the porch now in her underwear.

"Who said you could?" she said.

"Oh, come on, come on, come on, come on," Sam said, stuck on his own subject. "Let me," he said. "I'm an old hair braider from way back. Let me," he said to Alice, and then to her, "Please, you could be cute."

But the hair braids brought on more headache, and she went calling after George until she saw and woke him: George, pillowed on his own books now, cheek grooved with reading Chekhov. Ordinary life, she said, was so confusing, and George said, "Don't be ashamed."

She thought, He doesn't know me.

Sam was sucking on his pipe stem and turning up the violence on TV. "Fuck," he said, faulting her for acting intellectual. Every day—the rest of his life—Sam said he wanted to get high and fuck!

"Good luck," she said; but she had too much work to do to join him. She had a paper to write—this was college.

Days without sleep or food, she was locked in her room and writing papers. "Yes!" sometimes shouted when she read what she had written and approved of it: yes, yes, yes. The illusion of efficiency was easily heightened by the pills Alice gave her; and she was days awake and without appetite until, tearful and hungry, she gorged on junk snacks from the grocery. On its own, ready-made dip from the dairy section, she sucked it off her fingers—oh!

"Oh, I am so smart!" Sam said, all the time, to which she and Alice made faces.

They made faces at the faces George made whenever the three of them eavesdropped on Sam with a girl in bed. "Did anyone ever tell you how . . . how blue, how small." Her room was right next, so she rarely missed what Sam was doing in his, but the sounds of him depressed her, and Alice seemed glum, and George, tired.

The raft of George's room tossed in his door's opening.

She told him, "I'm bored or I'm lonely. I'm something. I don't know which, but Sam doesn't help." She went on talking about her mother and her problems with her mother. "George?" she asked then, wondering. He seemed to be staring at something he saw behind her when she spoke. He was at the window and the afternoon shone through him. His hair, she saw, stood up, surprised. He leaned against the windowsill, a wan, indoor, unembarrassed boy, and she wondered what George was doing in this house with them.

He was leaning in a stupor against Alice's long legs and laughing with the laughers on late-night shows.

He was smudging magazines with reading in the bath.

He was toking on the stoop and talking places he would travel.

Travel, the breezy takeoff, the names of Daddy's friends in case, dope in the tin box meant for mints—no, she said, this was not her Mexico. She said, "I was expecting pain, and I got it," and she told George how they were chased into the suburbs until the driver lost the threatening car and could slow past the houses. Harmless-looking houses, but inside one of them was the makeshift clinic where at dawn it began, and she was last. The abortionist! Girl after girl— some were women—walked in on her own to where the doctor did it, then was carried out knocked out, obscenely padded, elsewhere looseness, breasts and buttocks—ugly! Later, but not much later, quickly, in fact, they were dressed and in the kitchen before the driver took them back to the hotel. She said the pineapple they offered was freshly cut and juicy.

Everything she said came out like sex, which might have been the way she was or the way it was in the house.

But what was that genius George reciting wearing only a towel?

The death dates of important thinkers, the titles to their essays, and the size of their estates. Genealogies and distances, Latin mottoes, old boundaries, gonfalon flags, divisions of heraldry—partitions, ordinaries, charges, furs— were some of George's topics.

"Mary Moody Emerson slept in her shroud—took it on her travels—and wore out many."

"*Farther* has to do with distance, *further* has to do with more in time or degree."

"You're a better student than I am," he said to her, "but I am more ambitious." Later—much later, in fact—she thought how George had seduced her with this line, taking her seriously, acknowledging her efforts. She didn't even think of where he was standing when he spoke, looking in at her sudsing in the tub.

"Let me in," he said, scooping up a poof of foam with which he crowned her.

"No," she said, but he stepped out of his shorts and slipped in behind and put his hands beneath her breasts. He touched the pointy bones that were her hips, the swollen folds of her small sex.

"Stand up," he said.

"No," she said, laughing and at the same time rising to see her body fleeced with soap he blew away. Then George was pressing his fleshy mouth between her legs, and a part of her wondered if she was why George was living here in this swaybacked house miles from campus.

"Where's George?" Sam asked.

"My room," she said. "What's so funny about that?"

And nothing was funny about George sitting on old laundry—all sore knees and reddened elbows—and using his hand to ash what he smoked. Sam had rolled it for him.

"Fuck," she said, "fuck, fuck," while she tried to get George's attention. She shook him and asked, "Do you remember how many you took?"

Later, when George had slid off the laundry and was

using the floor as a bed, she wanted to know from Sam what George had swallowed. Was it anything like what they had had before? Then she was asking George. She was shaking him, exhorting—pleading, "Don't fall asleep!" but Alice, on the landing, said, "Fuck these boys."

Alice said, "You want to be careful. You don't think it happens, but it does." Alice, flicking stems and seeds from the resinous box between her legs, did not look up as she rolled thin cigarettes, laughing some, crying, saying, "You know how susceptible I am. I'll fuck anyone once," and then Alice said she was ashamed; and the plank between them broke, and she and Alice commiserated, "We're such dopes."

The messy intimacy of fucking aroused her, and she put down towels so as not to bleed through the sheets and told George, yes, some whiskey would do and fucking, yes, it helped, always, yes; but her bed was too jouncy and squeaky ridiculous for him, and there was the blood and a smell he could taste—a rusty taste, he said. He did and did not like it, so they quit.

George said, "I want to be happy more of the time than you are happy."

George said, "You are always going to have the problem of your mother."

George said, "And there's also your temper."

George said and he said and he said on the last afternoon when they picked at picnic food someone had made. The cheese was in a sweat, and the deviled eggs slimed off the dish, and the drink poured out flat and tasteless; but she drank and she ate and she fought off feeling sick. That was that.

The restless house rolled over hardly breathing, yet awake; and in this way it started. She and George. Alice and George. She and Alice and George. She and Alice and George and Sam. George and Sam. Sam and Alice. She and George again. She and Sam—but only once—and finally only Alice.

Fast past the wavy fields full of light and meaning—drive fast!

THE HUMAN SEASON

Monday and Monday and Monday pass, all ragged-sky and midday-sun sameness, all closets and drawers she stares into. None of what kept time once works.

Orlando!

She left home just as finally, then kept going back until she had found it: baby shoes, lace cap, scribble, and ribbons; what she was before she was, before otherness and memory. The nights without Orlando home go on.

"Don't even start!" Orin says, but she does. "It's always something wrong, goddammit!" Orin says, or else, "I'm exhausted."

Orin, no sweet name there, just ordinary, ornery, elbow-ugly Orin, asks if she has thought of something positive, say a movie. Tonight, tomorrow, he doesn't care—does she?

She shrugs and shrugs again when the movie is over, and Orin asks, "Whose idea was that?"

Earlier or later, the same night or any other, Orin asks, "Why did you bring me here?"

"You said you were hungry. Weren't you?" she asks.

Nights, Orin leaves to wake up in his bed downtown. Even now, with Orlando gone, Orin says he will not stay the night—don't ask him! Don't ask for any more money either; he does not have it! No more time for the Post House and Billy's or any of that overpriced Indian shit. The sweaters he has bought her, the shoes, the trips—what more does she want?

It has to do with her mouth, Orin, still sober, guesses.

"Yes," she says, excited.

"You're such a dirty girl," he says, but tonight he wants to drink.

Orlando, sweet Orlando, her boy, where is he calling from, what space of clanky sounds, many voices, music? "Are you drinking?" she asks.

No, he has called only to tell her this because it is amazing really, but it happened, just today he saw her, he saw his mother as she must have been once, on a school lawn, a girl with heavy eyebrows and a journal.

From where did he get this idea of her, from what photograph? How has Orlando imagined her, and is he the kind of boy to speak to the girl she was, and would she have talked to him? All the questions she might ask, but she lets Orlando talk.

She is so interested in him!

Orlando talks and talks. Of course he is keeping up; it's not all work here, hardly. Orlando says there is a girl.

Something about Orlando's voice—is it greener in Vermont?

Pretty college, place just rained on and swayed with water, his home now, where he lives, she has not been there. She says, "I'd like to see your room." The green beyond his window she imagines; birch bark, fogs, solitudes, this surely is the landscape where the poet walked. He, with his vigorous hair and worked hands, the farmer-poet in the photograph.

"I'd like to get away from earth awhile," Orlando says. "Yeah, it's all here."

Orlando again. This time, a little money, please, an advance on his allowance. "Don't worry," he assures. "I'm fine." Everything is nearly finished; he plans to come home after. He wants to bring a friend, okay?

"What do you think?" is her response although she does not—she does not!—want anyone else.

Orin says, "Spoiled bitch," when she shows him the phone bill. He reads, "October two, October three, four—what the hell was it that week?"

Clothes, books, teachers, the plans for Christmas that change. She wants to know what Orlando is doing, and so she calls him, and Orlando calls her, too; he calls collect, and they talk, and she imagines what he is doing and remembers what she did. Does anything change? She is a girl again and churning up spit to wash out the wine taste that sours her mouth. She wants to go home to a bath but is too afraid to say so, and she lets herself be fucked.

Orlando's girl sleeps under ironed sheets while his mother is used to the unwashed and defeated. His mother is used to the quiet in the late afternoon when she lies across his bed.

The muted TV is blinking action; the cold casserole is sunk—and she, she is undressing in Orlando's dark room; she is getting into his bed. Orlando's pillow smells of her from other nights.

Orin, in the near dark, she hears him slurring, "Go ahead, you sick bitch, rub yourself off on his sheets! I'm leaving!"

Does she sleep?

The next thing she knows, Orin is breaking a picture frame close to the bed. "Here's something for you to boohoo about," and he smashes the glass part and tears up the picture inside.

Who is it? She won't look.

Are the stars not yet damped when Orin, on the phone to poor Orlando, shouts, "Your mother is dead. Talk to me"?

"Orin, please, it's too late for that." The face she wears when she speaks is her youthful face from college. The long face isn't long but simply regretful; she is too young to be a young man's mother, too young for these abrasions— Orin's scorn. *Little* is the word he puts in front of what is hers.

Now there is only the mail, which mostly means writing checks. Pay to the order of doctor, doctor, doctor, doctor.

How many times a week does she go is what Orin wants to know.

But a lot of what happens she does not understand. That time Orin said he couldn't walk and made her call an ambulance, that time seemed incredible to her, and Orlando was at home, too. The boy was ten or eleven and saw what a drama could look like. Yelping obscenities, Orin was lifted, dragged, shoved onto, strapped in; he could not hold out his arms and snatch at what he passed riding through the house on a stretcher, shouting, "I'm in so much fucking pain!" Nothing could be found wrong, yet he got the pain pills for it, his crooked condition.

Confusions, she remembers, and embarrassments. Orin asleep at the dinner party and sick-drunk in the garden. "Orin, please," she was calling out softly, "not the hydrangeas."

The crystal, the chair—watch it!

Orin, uncomfortable in company, suspicious, loud, clumsy, in the habit of shouting, "Dim bulb, get me some ice"; Orin saying to Orlando, "Dim bulb, what do they teach you in that school?"; saying, "This kid is on another planet. I knew more at six." Nasty, nasty, Orin must have been a nasty child, the kind whose excuse for any cruelty was to see what would happen.

Orlando says, "Don't let Orin be there when I come. I don't want Isabel to meet him."

"Isabel," she says, so that's the friend's name.

She misses Orlando.

Light, ease, expectation, youth's surety, if she could only have it back. If she could have it back and be smarter. Stupid, she was stupid, swallowing pills before the purveyor explained them. She was tripping in the woods with no way home, stunned on the roof above the street fair. The girl she was sucked cock in cars until the head-on blare of air-conditioned air veered into violent headache. Why didn't she think to move? Stupid to be loudmouthed, loaded, stoned, to be passing cars when the sign says not to, to be fucking and fucking indifferent guys. No wonder she got into trouble. The gloom of the makeshift clinic, a row of cots and castered screens to close off those induced by drips, a woman's kind of suffering, she was not spared this, the mucousy consequence of fucking too freely. Stupid girl!

Orlando! She was smart enough at least to keep him.

The face in the reflective surface of the TV's screen is middle-aged and sly—her own face, talking. She is talking on the phone to Orlando, saying, "Think of what you'll miss if you don't visit. The lighting of the tree, the fireworks over the park." Rude surprise, this face she sees, but she keeps on looking at it, studying what happens as she talks and listens, until Orin turns the TV on and she disappears.

"Go fuck Sprint somewhere else!" he says.

The yarl of the sports announcer making his pitch, the shush of small confessions, advertisements, music.

"Whisper," she says to Orlando, then all they do is breathe. Close, long sounds—is he sighing? Orlando is at her ear, her ear pressed hard against the receiver, her burning ear into which he is pouring his sincere, sweet self!

"Come home," she says to the boy, "and bring your girl."

"I don't want there to be a fight," Orlando says, and she tells him there won't be, just watch.

Watch the way the drinking works on Orin's body, a bag of sand sagged in the easy chair, bobbing in the sprung-seated easy chair, a shapeless shape, a clay pale, a damp face, a man drunk on vodka, the bottle of which he keeps at hand.

The foamy spittle in the corners of his mouth repels her.

Maybe Orlando should stay at a friend's, maybe he is right when he says home's too dangerous.

"Only think about it," she says to the boy.

Orin, in the background, is the scary noise.

Orlando says, "No, I can't, not this time."

And not when the new growth pinks the slick branches, not in spring, when Orlando needs sleep.

He says, "Mother, think."

She thinks of the constant sounds from year to year, the machinery's wail in summer and in the fall the sound of children from the next-door school. The piercing nag, the way the bully rules—such certitude!—children talking, endlessly talking. They have so much to say. Winter, then, the inward month; in winter the sounds are close.

The sounds are of heat roiling from the radiators, creaks from the furniture, pipes. She likes these house sounds that go on until the weather changes, and the windows are opened, and it is spring, and summer is about to happen again.

Listen!

The future in her ears comes out like this.

THE LIFE OF THE PALM
AND THE BREAST

The mirror, the mirror untethers the room and sets it afloat above the park. The mirror makes her tipsy, and perhaps she is tipsy here, turning to look out at the winter sky and shy black skyline, out at a dainty city with the lights come softly on. Such pleasures! The views from a building secure as a banker in his snug, plush coat—there is so much to be pleased by.

There is the flawless father who pleases her and the washed windows that front the seeping dark and pearly dusk. Inside, the colors she has picked are deep and expensive. Reds, blues. The fire is lit and the damp balsam, twisted up with spruce and draped along the mantel, smells green. Speckled pears, nuts, oranges—even a grapefruit—color the garland and double in the mirror they partly frame. No wonder she is dizzy.

Little boys are running through the room in velvet shorts. She cannot tell which boys are hers; they are so look-alike, she hesitates to take one.

"You?" The small neck pulses in her grip. There is, too, the familiar wet mouth, the cheeks, winter chapped and warm, the child-pungent hair she puts her face to.

The little boys at night in bed, they smell of soap the sheets are washed in; but in the morning, salty.

SPRING

The guests have gone and the children are asleep and the au pair is drying the dishes when she invites the flawless father, the same she calls by many other names and all of them endearing, she invites the flawless man for a walk outside. Just up and down a few of her favorite blocks, under the fringe of pear trees. The streetlights make a lace of their blossoms.

"We live in a pretty neighborhood," she says, and he agrees.

The little boys use their Sunday palm as whips while the girl cousins quietly flank him, this father, her lover—their uncle!—the faithful man who promises the boys won't, no, not to the girls they will not. "Boys!" is all he says, and the boys drag their fronds like sticks across the fencing.

The park side of the street is guttered with elm seeds, and the catkins she points out, aren't they sexy?

The shy grace of new flowers in clean skirts, spring it is, yes, and the bare, skinned morning, opening slowly, seems to shiver.

"Yes," she says in the tremulous light of late spring, Sunday, late, the children far below on the street at the park in the part of Sunday that is theirs, when she can walk through the kitchen undressed and calling to him, "What else would you like to eat?"

The flawless man says he would know where to find her on any afternoon, but his voice still comes as a surprise when the manicurist holds the phone to her ear, and she hears him ask, "Can you be ready for Paris—in an hour?"

Oh, it is fun to be rich and darling!

Wedding linen, cut flowers, drawers that shut soundly. The silver nestled in felt bags, passed-down pieces, tarnished spoons, she warms them in her hands. Mother Pet's initialed tongs, the berry spoon from Nana.

It is always this way before a party, isn't it? The dead are moving their mouths when the living come slamming in. "Back so soon?" she asks the boys. Caught in the spring rain, caught before lunch, the flawless father and the flawless boys are come back long before expected. "Stay away from me! Stay where you are," she says. Stay there beyond the kitchen, where the muddy boots pant and lacrosse sticks drip wetly.

"You're not still in Bermuda" is what she says to the boys when they sock-slide in the kitchen half undressed. Their bodies are tanned; only the flawless father isn't peeling. His shoulders are hairless and smooth and freckled with runny freckles. She feels if the freckles are raised, and she feels how warm he is and keeps her hand at his back while he asks her who exactly is coming.

Pansy, Daphne, Lily, Georgia.

The young women friends, yes, he likes them—he likes all women, really, but these washed wands in small clothes especially! They are all legs and arms and don't stand still to talk but rock on their hips and gesture. "Sorry, sorry, sorry," they say. They are late but they are eager. Even if they swing in on crutches with their own young husbands just behind, the young women are jaunty. She watches from across the room how the young women surprise themselves with what they say to him.

First lilac, everywhere. Smell.

SUMMER

"Whatever you want," he says. "I'm painting."

The ceremonies are over; it is summer and he is painting. Hatless, shirtless, he is on the ladder rolling paint on the mildewed cottage ceiling. Paint catches in his hair and in the hair on his arms and in the saddle of his back. He is paint-flecked with a color called French white. He is pollinated, a flower, dusted.

Look at him, the way the paint washes off in the water's blast, swashing down his face, his malleable face, the tolerant mouth turned up at the ends, the eyes that when he smiles pleat sweetly—no other word for it. He is such a boy. The way he is about water, how he likes to stand in it.

The waters off Penobscot are sun chinked and cold; nothing skits the surface that might bite. The surface is a mirror to mirror the spruce tipped toward it, and the pink-cliffed shoreline blushes deeply. At sunset he swims. His heavy arms break water. His heavy, lifting arms are mostly water, and the water is cold; she has felt it; and when he wobbles out of the water over the mussel-stuccoed shore, he makes the noise of someone cold. He huffs and grins at what he has just done.

But what he has not done! He has not finished . . . and not finished, not finished reading *Ulysses* or even started the Thoreau. He is wall building in the garden still; he is walking the island, going out in the boat. "See where he is?" She points for the children. "He is at the water after stones for the wall." See? He hefts a stone on his shoulder and holds another at his hip up the hill to the low wall with its band of black-eyed Susans.

How is it he carries these stones but easily, lightly? Oh, he is so perfectly good! He is the way, she thinks, a hero should be.

FALL

Late August—is summer so short and over? It is cold enough this morning for a fire! The rain clouds the fields, and the blown fog boils until they leave the cottage and it lifts. "Can you see?" she asks. The barrens have begun to redden, and the goldenrod wags gold.

Oh, snatch past reds that in passing smear! Shut your eyes on the sumac!

"Go fast," say the children when the sudden road cleared invites them.

The flawless man's hands and his arms and the hair on his arms, she takes pleasure in the sight of his arms when he is driving them back to the onrush of the city—September, October, November! Binders, apples, pencils, socks—so fast and already they are home, home, where an unexpected face she wears streaks past familiar mirrors and dismays her. Although he says ... he says such things—oh, it embarrasses her what the flawless man says, and she wants to believe him. She does believe him!

Of equable temperament, generous, upright, faithful, kind: the flawless father, lover, friend is all of these; and his hands, turned outward, are cupped for her. Yes, she likes to be done to, she likes to be bossed and made to feel what she feels—fleshy, cleft, insatiable, a bit of a tramp on the spit of his hand, the same hand deft enough to catch in passing a doll the boys have twisted into splits.

He swipes up the doll—so much hair on a stick—and ever the flawless uncle, he shuts the doll's legs and smooths her dress and says to the owner, "Avoid the boys. Come sit by the fire and play near us," and when the girl goes home, the boys take her place and loll by the heat on their bellies, pushing trucks. The fire stuns them. Their cheeks are flushed, and when she finger combs their hair, their hair is wet. "Go to bed," she says, and the flawless father walks them.

Falling and falling all night into sleep, the boys are noisy breathers and kick at their covers.

How has it happened they have these boys is something she likes to say, and she says it, walking to where he is sitting in front of the fire, "How is it we . . . ?" So much of what she says at night goes unfinished. She would rather kiss and be kissed and watch the soft collapse of cindered logs in the darkening room where they are themselves greater darknesses, touching.

WINTER

Lap robes and cushions and candlesticks, greenery and oranges, spiky flowers, rows of things red, silver bowls of

Christmas bulbs, decorations made of candies, these are some of the jammy comforts attached to this time when radiator heat squiggles palpably and whitely in the room. "Aren't you thirsty?" she asks the flawless father, and she asks the boys; but the boys go on gouging chocolates and sucking out the cherries. Their lips, when she licks them, are sweet.

And other parts of them are sweet. The pocked baby parts of their hands, the sugared wells between their fingers, the boys are grooved for licking and taste good.

What makes her so special except that she is, yes, surely, look at the unfolded body the flawless man helps her keep: how he comes up from behind her, and the urgent first abrasive pleasure is a pleasure she would like to repeat even as it happens, so that she does. Her body flashes in the mirrored door where the city floats in the white light of winter, in the pink of spring, soft June, the heat wave that shrivels, August, October; the city wakes, rises, backdrops the dark head pressed against her breast.

Is it any wonder she is dizzy?

Shouldn't she be afraid?

THEY TURN THEIR BODIES
INTO SPEARS

I

On the first night they took her to the locals' favorite for
lobster, she got sick, and they consoled her home with excuses. It must have been the boat to the island and the egg-
white scum that spilled from the claws when she cracked
them. It must have been the distance she had traveled to
visit. Imagine their surprise! Suddenly their daughter's girl
knocking open the screen door, carrying a string bag of
oranges, a few clothes, and some tapes, no plans, but an
appetite, it seemed, for what the island fetched up in traps.
Lobster, her favorite, although the face she wore on their
walk back home was cast down and waxy. Ellen put her to
bed while he looked at the sky and thought how sad a girl
could be at twenty.

He was eighty. He had lived long enough to see the
children's children shrivel into age, and he wanted to tell
his granddaughter what it meant, really, to be eighty and
alive.

"That old!" she gasped when in the morning they
spoke.

"Yes, I am, and I know things. Be happy. Don't wait."

He struck up the fire and stayed squatted to watch it take; in the kitchen Ellen frittered at their breakfast. Eat, drink. This was a treat for them, Ellen was saying; it was not every day their granddaughter visited, and they were happy to see her. Happy again, the word sprung wild as the island's regal wagging, fields of weedy purples and golds, red geraniums against the chalky houses. Their umpteenth summer here alone, his and Ellen's, and they woke to the weather, pleasure bent.

Old folks' pleasure, maybe; maybe that was what the girl would call it. Seed-dry and slow—too many books, no TV; birds their only entertainment. Old folks they were with old folks' ways. The temperature's night plummet meant it was cold when they awoke, and he often made a fire.

He had been laying kindling when the girl scuffed in, wearing a blanket—no robe—next morning.

"Charlotte!" Ellen said. "Aren't you cold?"

No, thank you, yes, thank you, no was his granddaughter speaking—the darling! Look at the bits of cloth she wore when she was dressed. No breasts. Jutted movement, bones—her bones, Charlotte's—were handles, too visible. She had what so many girls had that made them turn their bodies into spears. Wing blades and wrist bones, bones, bones, a girl distinctly outlined, her eyes were fixed on the water.

"I haven't been here in such a long time," she said.

He reminded her of what she needed to know if she should go out in the boat. The cove. The lily pond. The ledge where the eagles nested.

They kept the house door unlocked.

"Crime is everywhere, Poppie. Even here," she said, but he laughed.

He said, "You don't need to drive anywhere, but I trust you with the car." He said this although he wasn't sure. Never had he seen the girl off but he thought she would fail. This girl, he thought, was so much like his daughter, and he watched as she swayed down the path swapping branches. Was she talking to herself?

II

Charlotte said her mother always expected to see a prettier daughter. This was on the porch, when they sat, the three of them, in the morning and watched the waves in their halfhearted slash against the shore.

Ellen said, "You mustn't listen to your mother. She doesn't know what she is saying."

"I know," Charlotte said. "Mom's just being mean."

"She is," Ellen said and she put her arms around the girl and told her how pretty she was and how much loved.

Charlotte, cheered, told stories about her mother. "Mother says she is a very good camper." Charlotte made a sound, a little like a laugh, but then, it seemed, she saw what he saw and, made afraid, turned quiet.

III

He thought umpteen years when he calculated time on the island with only his wife, but in total, as a family, it was fifty years—hardly umpteen—summer after summer in the cranky rusticator, brambled, slanted, bleached. Dishes of opened mussel shells blued the bathroom vanities, stones from the beach held back books. Faded top sheets in sea-glass colors—green, blue, yellow, pink—lifted in the wind unanchored by the blankets Ellen kept in chests. After breakfast every morning Ellen opened the bedroom windows wide to the sea and aired the house even as he nudged the fire downstairs. Years with and without a daughter. Without a daughter had been better.

"Your grandmother and I are here to be happy," he said when Ellen was gone with her basket and shears. He said, "Try to be happy yourself while you're here," and he walked off the porch toward the water. If his knees could be oiled, he thought, he might reach the shore faster.

IV

"This is serious," Charlotte said, and she lolled on the dock with him and talked about school and her father and the Wilderness Defense and her father (again) and the criminal amounts of money made on Wall Street. "I mean I'm glad for Daddy and all, but there are too many poor people in the country."

"Swim!" he said. "The water is not so cold."

V

Lunch, and he told the girl to eat her pickle before he did. What he loved about the girl were her girlish ways. How she broke up a muffin to find the berries and pelleted the cakey crumbs to feed the chickadees, the way she called to all living things in a clear voice, he loved this much about her, and the way she licked her lips or twisted her hair when she was thinking. Her far-off face when she was thinking, her ardent, flushed face. The shallow pan of breastbone, her close, pretty ear. Darling girl, his darling, he confused her sometimes with his daughter.

Ellen was saying, "They have said they will call us when they think we can visit your mother."

He wished his granddaughter had gone somewhere else

to rest. He wanted no more stories about his daughter. He was too old. Old, sick, set back by the same news that his daughter was not happy.

"That's the least of it," Ellen said.

"I was tired last night, Poppie, if that's what you mean. I don't get sick often."

He asked, "So why don't you eat instead of picking?" How he must look to her—beaked, lidded, wattled, a moody old man with shames and losses, very few friends, no hobbies. Crabbed, sullen, closed off, failed. All he had done was make money, money, money, enough to buy a summerhouse when he was yet young and then old, old for a long time, long enough for his daughter to squander lots of it—money.

He said, "You'd do well to think of what's happened to her." He was about to say more when Charlotte began to cry.

VI

How he had found his bedroom, he could not remember, but the sun through the trees stippled the blanket that covered him, and he knew, at least, that it was late afternoon, the bay calmed, the water too blue and sun scratched to look at. He knew he had slept and that the shrill part of the day was over; the house was very quiet. The quiet of the wholly present tense, the luxurious absence of melancholy, ire, and whatever other meanness switched him through the house, all was easy and now. Now and now and now. He stepped onto the porch with a dish of peanuts and his drink, his glasses, his book. Heart's ease at dusk, the sky orange edged at first, then "Ellen!" he was calling. "You're missing this. Come look!" But she was already just behind him, humming approvingly at the plummy clouds.

But here she comes, blooded with sunset, his daughter and his granddaughter. His granddaughter saying, "It's all right, Poppie. There's no reason to be sad."

"Jimmy," Ellen said, "Charlotte is asking you a question," and she was shaking him back to the porch and the girl who was grown.

His daughter is combing with her fingers what is left of her hair. Her face is flat against a screen. She is talking but he doesn't know about what.

See the candles, the cake.

Balloons, brushed against, snap, and her fine hair stands on end, and her black patent leather shoes make staticky cracks, and a little girl cries, "They bite!"

The sunburn that had put him to sleep woke him to his

wife asking, "Are you cold, dear?" saying, "Charlotte, darling, get Poppie his jacket, will you?"

"I'm not hungry," he said. "I feel sick."

VII

Ellen brought him beef broth and would gladly have sat
on the next bed watching if he hadn't said, "Go on, go on,
go on," and when Ellen asked again "Are you sure . . . ?"
he frowned at her until the door shut softly and she was
gone.

He slept. His dreams closed abruptly, and he woke at
spooky no-man's-hours and stayed awake until the shape
he knew for his wife became his wife. The room cohered.
The table, the dresser, the lamp, the rug seemed no longer
some dead man's effects, and he stood, whole and unen-
cumbered, watching the glaucous outdoor colors deepen.
A windless hour and he could hear, or thought he could
hear, the gurgle of low-tide muck, its stinky, hissing bounty.

He had had a daughter once. She picked the shore to
fill glass globes with decorative reminders of the sea. Ever
a brooder, weeping over the unretrievable summer, she let
the anger rise in her, like tide, until it brimmed and spilled
and ended in showy injuries, smashing the glass globes
against the bathroom tiles and walking through the house
in bloody feet.

The morning yellowed and he was well again and picked his way to the granite shelf that in the light had dried. Here he sat, for a long time sat, proudly agile, an old, old man—eighty!—in only a flannel robe, thin pajamas, and boiled wool slippers, all gifts his wife insisted on. "Wear them, Jimmy, or you'll catch your death of cold!"

"Poppie!"

Charlotte, he saw, was zigzagging toward him, happy. "Poppie! Granmum says to come in and get warm."

VIII

"Ellen, Ellen, Ellen, for God's sake, please!" He was looking in the bird book for what had flown overhead.

He wouldn't look at Ellen and he turned away from her in his chair, away from Charlotte, too. The girl took up so much room. "You've been on the phone for hours, Charlotte!" he said. Her cheerful response was unwelcome.

"Poppie!" she said and then piping sounds into the phone.

"Get off the phone, Charlotte. Now," he said and he was standing. He was looking right at her and she was smiling.

She hung up the phone and waved a notepad and said, "This is my trip to Boston, Granmum. I'll leave it here for now."

He knew the kind of Kleenex crud a crying girl left behind. Notepads and numbers on notepads, numbers turned fat with writing over and over them, and over names and other numbers, cars, flights, addresses. He had found such wreckage before and called to his wife, "What is this?"

SEE AMID THE WINTER'S SNOW

1986

Once their faces easily pinked in the Christmas gaudy. Toy-mad and dithered, the boys at Christmas, running out of close parties and open to the wind. We crossed to walk the park side and looked up through the trees to see the sky was turned to firmament; the stars to ancient purpose; nothing was as it was, but indwelling spirit swelled and fat with Christmas. Mother buttered strudel and cried for no occasion except that they were gone, NettaandDaddy, her own, who used to have, who used to do, who always something-something at this time of year. Mother cried for me and for the boys and for my sister (who would not forgive her).

"But what have I done?" In the tunnels of tree stands, she cried, and at the first snow, and sometimes when the boys brushed against her, and always when the boys sang. Her tears delighted them. "Nana's crying! Nana's crying! Nana's crying, Mother!"

"Mother," I said, "come help me," and she watched from a stool as I toothbrushed the silver.

"Who besides us is coming?" she asked.

"No one, no; and no to that question, too." No, I am not. He did not, we never. She did not understand why I didn't take him to court or why my in-laws kept their money or why I bothered to bake. What did she raise in me, my mother, except such disappointment that all I could do was rush from the kitchen and put on the music that made me feel holy and sad and slightly foolish? "Personent Hodie," thumped and vigorous, embarrassed me, but "See amid the Winter's Snow" was quieting, and Mother sipped her drink. I didn't mind then the hard light, bright as any snowfield and flaring off the buildings our windows faced; I could stand to look hearing little-boy church voices vaulted in the background.

The boys were in the background, too; my own, and Mother's, these boys talking for the toys they moved in battles sounded through the afternoon. The pursed, soured, shrunk about our lives, Mother's as much as mine, fell away when the radiators shushed and spit and we were safe.

Where were the boys then just before Christmas?

Who would sugar the cookies?

Mother lay in bed and read whatever had taken her fancy in the airport: the royals this Christmas with their corgis at Balmoral—look! Mother wanted to live in a castle just like that—and why not? Didn't she deserve it? Mother using up the bubbles in her afternoon ablutions. Mother was a red fragrance, profligately splashed. Her suitcase and the silky lingerie she packed were acrid with the mixed-up smell of her and her perfume and what she drank.

What did she bring that was new this time?

Less and less, the same and the favorites, lace ripped and straps thinned. Nothing to borrow . . . single earrings and unstrung pearls, dulled rings home mended with Band-Aids . . . grit in the boxes she used to case them, her jewels, as Mother called them. Her jewels or her sparkles . . . "Oh, what a Sparkle Plenty you are! Darling!" Mother was belling the cat with us now for how many Christmases? "Count," and Mother did. "That was the year your father, your husband, my ex-husband, your ex-husband, the ugly boyfriend—who was he?"

"Mother, please, can we talk of something else, please."

The snow tracks fast filling in with falling snow, winter solstice in the Sheraton Avenue house, where she sat at the top of the staircase and saw her handsome brothers off. Black mufflers, camel coats, lustrous patent leather dancing shoes, her brothers in formal dress. Mother said she saw them from the staircase and from the landing's window sliding on those shoes, boys still, in and out of light. Good-bye! She huffed at the window to make a smoke to draw in, but the ring came out small and her mark disappeared.

"You dasn't" was how the maid said no to Mother. "You

dasn't go in your brothers' rooms when they are out." My mother went in anyway, but looking for what?

"I wanted to be surprised," Mother said. "I was nosy. Even when I knew what it was in a drawer, I opened it."

I was also that way. For a long time, even after I knew the contents, I opened Mother's house; but she didn't bother to look through my rooms anymore. In powdered undress she sat on the edge of my bed and said, "So this is Christmas."

My sentiments exactly when the boys were gone, although there was tonight with the boys at the theater— her treat. "Remember?"

She had almost forgotten.

She said, "I don't feel well today," and she went back to bed with a littleglassofsomething, as she called it. She wanted to take advantage of the quiet and for a while to shut her eyes, to clear her head, to think of other things besides Christmas. Mother said, "I have no business buying theater tickets, but I'm glad I did, of course, for the boys. The boys should get to see good theater—only the expense of it!" Money, money, money, the icy blast of Christmas through the rotted sash. I had felt that chill before and longed for bed.

"Want more to drink?" I asked.

"You are so much like me," Mother said, holding out her glass.

I hoped not, but I was.

I was rushing bacon and using too much soap on pans; whatever I cooked in them came out tasting soapy. "I can't eat this, Mom," from a boy. Me, forgetting and forgetting or getting there late. "Mom!" I was full of apology but unprepared. Whoever carried safety pins and never got lost? "I will make it work, I will make it work, be patient." The boys did not believe me any more than I believed my mother when she said, "I promise." Mother promised Rollerblades for Christmas; for the other boy, Australia. Mother said to me, "When he is twenty-one, I am taking him."

"Does it snow in Australia?" he asked, come home and out of the sky's new falling and already anxious to be gone again and released and dangerous and loud.

"Be quiet," I said. "Both of you. Nana is resting."

But Nana was calling to them, and if she was resting, then why was she talking?

They went on asking, "Nana?" walking into her room, trailing gifts from Dad to show but running out before they did.

"Nana's crying, Mother!" from both boys in excited voices. "Nana's crying!"

The stink of old-lady perfume, and Mother, an old lady, crying over it. "Not broken, only spilled," I assured her, "and only a little spilled, all right then, enough to wear and not to cry over, Mother." I righted the empty glass and set the clock back so she could better see it.

"Your sister has always been so angry," Mother said to me, and she was crying again because we should have been together. "We're too few as it is," she said. "She should be here and her husband and those children. They don't even know me. What are their names? You see, I forget. This is not my idea of Christmas."

I reminded her about the theater and said tomorrow Frannie would call.

But NettaandDaddy, NettaandDaddy doused the plum pudding and put it aflame.

I said, "Your drink, Mother, here."

"Your sister," she said, sipping. "I don't dare around her."

Mother grunted off her bathrobe and trembled down the hall in just her nylons and brassiere. She said, "What are you going to wear?" and she watched me dress and wondered when it happened she got old, and I was old, too, she assured me, and my sister was older than both of us. Mother said, "Daddy wasn't so very old when he died, yet poor Daddy. They would not let me see him. They didn't even call in time for me to see him. They just put him in the ground. I found out later."

"Mother . . ."

"See how you like it. See what it feels like . . . lost, and now you have to worry."

"Mother. . . ."

She was trying on my perfumes and asking, "Local?"

"Cheap," I answered. I said yesandno to everything else she asked me. It is not as it was with NettaandDaddy; we will never again. "Give me," I said and took her drink and snuffed the fumes and thought I would catch fire.

"Outside," I said, "it looks like Christmas," and it did. The snow, expected but turned larger, sifted in the wind and worked its intimate diminishment. Only the sky was left to see and violet-colored, lavish flakes falling on our tongues. Aahhhhhhh at the heavens running backward and Mother repeating, "I don't dare fall. If I fall . . ." The boys said they would catch her. Then the snow's assaulting angle sharpened, and it stormed, and we couldn't see the sky, and Mother was crying. She was very, very drunk by then, and it came as no surprise to me that she fell at a curb, almost at the theater, amidst a host of people. Mother fell on her knees, and I let strangers help her.

1996

Yes, I think, yes, we are smiling at the missing boy's smile, my mother and I, in the last room, low, north facing, dark, with harsh, budget carpet and trunklike furniture that a

janitor bangs into with his cart—ouch! Over the noise of
running water and, later, the vacuum, I shout at Mother,
and I pretend that he is here, sixteen and shirtless, straight-
ened teeth, the missing boy my mother says isn't a baby
anymore, is he?

The next time we are smiling at a boy for real, a grandson
bending to his grandmother's chair. Heartbreaker is what
he is, and my mother says, "Yes," and she touches his wrist.
That point of grace or seriousness or whatever the boy's
wrist bone suggests, it is there that she touches him.

The white band of skin is from his watch.

Why no watch? I wonder. Where is it?

"Hello, Nana."

"Louder," I instruct.

"Hello, Nana!"

His hand, his shapely hand, is a ruddy reminder of
health against the pale summer blanket Mother wears like
swaddling. He turns out his hands, and Mother takes them
to her face and smells. June, the white-flower month, ripe
privet greens the air, and the palm against my mother's
face, I guess, must smell as sweet. I listen to her breathe
him in. Her breathing is a screechy hinge to a garden my
mother would speak of, her own. The garden is behind and
around my mother; sun patches the floor—and the light!
But the sound she makes makes me think how clean the

boy must smell in a season not yet noon when Mother will be—how old will Mother be? Where is she?

Today she is in school. Today the ambulatory are teachers, and Mother must apologize for being late—again!—with homework. This is a visit we make in the summer, when the boy's school is not in session.

"I perused the books," Mother says. Then in a voice that suggests there might be spies punitively near, Mother whispers how she misses, misses her children; but after lunch Mother says, "Why be so fussy!" Mother's eyes don't go along with her smile. Is she in there looking out her eye-holes at me?

"Mother?"

"You are older," Mother says to me. "Oh, but you look so old!"

I am surprised, too, surprised to be as old as women once hard for me to look at.

Dressed in a blanket at table 3, Mother says, "Surprise me," and she lets herself be fed. "I know peas," Mother says, now lighthearted. "I'm hungry."

"You are older," Mother says to me after what has just passed for lunch. "Oh, but you look so old!" To the boy, suddenly evident, she says, "Come closer," and he does. He bends close enough for her to touch his shoulder.

His shoulder and his arms are firmly shaped, and as with every part of him—his teeth, his skin—he is unmarked and smooth. He might take anything on—he could carry his nana!

"So she can see you," I say, and the boy is on his knees close enough for her to touch his shoulder, but she touches his nipple instead.

"Mom!" he says.

I keep my mouth shut so tightly my teeth hurt. Don't ask me why. I say, "Take up her hand and squeeze it tight."

When this boy frowns, he looks like his older brother.

Mother, in her chair, says she can drive around, too, and I curl on the floor at her feet like a dog and sleep. When I wake, Mother and I are at the top of a sloping lawn that meadows to a lake. Mother is talking to her mother about the rain: how the lake is high from it, rain and more rain. The rains bruise the ruffled flowers. The lake is black.

Now in our dream comes more rain; it peens the water colorless.

Now a white sky and commonly blue water, and now black water, choppy. I think I hear the neighbors jumping in off the dock.

"Agnes!" someone cries, and Mother startles. "It's a bird." The snake has eaten its eggs, she explains, and we must be careful. Mother says, "Be careful. These aren't just grass snakes but something bigger," and she holds up her little feet in immaculately white canvas sneakers.

Mother's snakes, once they slither into her story, they stay, and their slime, she says, is like snot, and it sickens her, really, and she gags. She leans over the chair and spits up all the peas she ate.

I am glad the boy is not here to see the depressant clarity of the unused, the way they wipe down the rooms here and swipe at the blinds. I wonder, Does Mother notice? The tightly rigged bed bleeps alarm: just my purse against the pillow sets it off.

A nurse strides in and scolds, "Again!"

I am curled at Mother's feet like a dog when here is a nurse asking, "What are you doing?"

"This is the safest place to sleep," I say. "The bed rings."

Oh, this is no birdcage, Mother's nursing home, not the birdcage she liked in La Jolla, with its patio views of the ocean. That unobstructed tower in the sun, does she remember it, the one I think she planned on and often pointed to, saying, "That's where the gray ladies perch."

Thank heavens the boy is not here to hear us sighing into a gaze over something of his. Today I have the boy's books, paperbacks mostly, but this one—look! Chemistry! The split spine has loosed its cover; the cover wags like a tooth from how he worried it. Clearly, the book has been handled; clearly, he worked. "Like you, Mother," I say, "he wants to be a good student."

Mother says, "I am."

Mother turns the missing boy's watch cap inside out to where the dark spice of his scalp is strongest. I know; I have smelled it and felt, too, the wet wool between my fingers and thought, How itchy it must be. And, Why does he wear it?

With the watch cap at her mouth, can Mother see him?

Hooded in a sweatshirt, he stands with his thumped fists pushing out his pockets. He rocks on his feet; his eyes are shut, water drips from his nose. The boy might be this way to her or in the back row of class, a goof-off with his watch cap on, captioning lewd drawings, or maybe she sees the long slide of his legs stuck out to trip up his friend.

"How did he get to be so unattractive!" she asks. "How did he?"

The boy? I am outraged. I am thinking, You, you are unattractive, Mother.

What did she expect? Of course, this is not the boy who ran steeply in circles on the field that was the beach when the tide was out, but he is still a pleasure to look at.

Take up the hankie weight of his shapely T-shirt, the washed sock, the sticky handle to his racket, and he might be seen as he was some afternoons when he skidded on the court or, later, when his wet hair was combed back and blackly curling at his ear.

Take up the hoop he wears. Is the post still warm, or the strap to his watch? (His watch, at least, is not lost!) The graduation gifts, see them? The watch again, the pen, the unpolished buckle decoratively scored and darkly initialed. A girl's name gouged in his journal cover, the journal from the suitcase I have brought of things to show Mother because he will not come, not today at least. Here is a braided bracelet from the summer, a stained bandanna. What does Mother know of him, the boy who is missing, except what I put into her hands? The boy's blue shirt, ironed spineless as a towel, I put the boy's shirt into Mother's hands.

All the missing boys, we miss them.

"He is not a baby anymore," Mother says.

"No, no," and not so young, and hardly dutiful, though I have wished. I have wished for his company through the watery heat I have had to wade through just to get here.

Mother's room is north facing; the inside air is cold.

2000

Our mother is living in the home state again in the dead-end part of one of those places for when there are no other places but this, a tiled corridor bristling with obstruction, idlers in slippers, uncomfortable chairs, carts, screens, trays, lids. Every door is open, even to the lady who shouts.

Mother, I don't think, shouts; but Faye on the night shift says that she hits. In the last few days Mother has grown more bewildered, and she doesn't want to go to bed. Faye has told me Mother says she has given up looking for us. Mother says her girls are with Netta and Daddy at the lake. Netta and Daddy are taking care of us.

I saw our mother in June, my sister saw her in October, but both times all our mother talked about was home, the one Mother had with Netta and Daddy on the lake. Our mother talks of the lake; she talks of lawns and elms around her—elms not yet sick. Mother grew up in the shade of these in a house with help, a cook, a baker, a laundress, old Peter, who just raked the leaves. The house looked out to the lake, the one she talks about now, asking, "Are you out at the lake? Have you seen Netta and Daddy?"

We don't understand it. Why, if our mother has released herself to wander, can't Mother wander near the ocean? The ocean brought skies that soothed her. "Oh, look at the size of those clouds!" Mother would say. "Will you look at the size of those clouds!" Spacious, God-blown clouds they were, and we spent a lot of time looking up.

So why did we bring Mother to the downward look of home, except that she is nearer home? Our mother is back in the home state, where the winters are so long. The sky, too, is not much to look at; and the lake, Mother's lake, is severe—very deep. Her lake, we remember, is silty, unusually dark, a green almost blue, and in no way like the lakes across the road. Those lakes in this land of lakes are shallow enough to be yellow. Some are swamps; mosquitoes appear on the first warm breath. September, October, November. Mosquitoes dangling over the pumpkin gore, Indian summer, it is easy to be stung then. Common in March and April to see the insects' soft appearance, or to walk through snows and snow fogs in May, to fan our underarms in August heat come in early June. Spring in the home state is often no spring at all. Summer is changeable, humid as a mouth sometimes or parched.

Look out the window. See for yourself.

"Look out the window, Agnes!" is what Faye says she says to our mother, but our mother stares at her lap. Her head, Mother says, is too heavy to lift. Besides, she has seen it. She knows where she is. Mother is belted in her chair and slumped. The nurses keep her parked near the station, where she hides behind her hair and barks. She will talk only in her room. She will talk about the lake. She will cry. "Tell Netta and Daddy we are never to be apart again. Camp is almost over."

A ringing phone confuses her unless it's held against

her ear, then Mother knows to talk. She asks, "Are you out at the lake? Will you send old Peter for me? I want to go out with Daddy in the Shepherd and watch the race."

This Mother is sixteen again and rocking in the mahogany chest Daddy calls the Shepherd. The warmed leather seat where she sits in the back puts her to sleep, that and the rocking motion of the boat against the pier, because Daddy is not yet ready to let Agnes's older brother cast off.

"What the hell do you think you're doing?" Daddy is always mad at the grown-up sons, the brothers; but Agnes, Daddy adores. She is only Daddy's no matter what that Netta says. Netta is the one who doesn't belong. She is jealous of what Agnes can do. Agnes can swim and so be with Daddy; poor Netta never learned how.

On the porch and sitting sternly, Netta does needlework that strains her eyes; she sits with her back to the pier, preferring a view of the garden.

The pier, the lake, that part of the estate removed from Netta, is where Agnes spends most of her time. The pier is not so long as it is wide. There is a floating dock Agnes swims to, or else on the pier she puts a project between her legs and glues or paints. Agnes starts before the pier is in the sun, when it is cold yet and wet underfoot; the water soaks the first layer of newspaper she lays to work on. The backs of her oiled legs are inky, and her sticky fingertips catch in her hair. Her hair! Her hair is a spun sugar, a matter of light, fine as glass and a white blond—even between her legs.

Oh, put your hand to it now, feel!

Agnes is aflame, and flammable with such fair skin, she uses an umbrella in the sun.

Is it any wonder then that Daddy wants her in his boat? To keep an eye on her and hold off boys.

Agnes's spun-sugar hair, her white-blond hair, whiskers her breasts when she bends to her work. "Not bad," she says, appraising what she has done, "but I should have, I should have . . ." Her jealous mother on the porch agrees. Her jealous mother calls the work dashed off and nothing serious.

Agnes is sixteen, and her chest shows a cleft when she bends, and there, between her breasts, Agnes sweats.

After forty, she will have no desires.

My sister and I hold the phone to our ears and breathe. We talk about Mother and the drapery of her skin, for instance, and what's between her legs.

We think of our legs, too, each of us, alone; I can hear how we breathe; I know.

We are lucky to live far away. We don't have to see our mother. We can get reports from Faye.

Faye says, "Yesterday it was horses. In the stable next door a boy was crying because his horse had died."

I wonder—my sister wonders—How did Mother find dead horses?

Faye says, "Remember how old she is."

Our mother, talking at the phone, is purely sixteen. Agnes is sixteen years old and talking boys, always boys. Always it is the boys with her, that is what Agnes's jealous mother on the porch says. "Always boys," she is muttering. "Agnes . . . we're going to . . ." Oh, that jealous mother's shadowed face is witchy. Just look! Look at her! Under a light made for handiwork, Agnes's mother is beading sweaters. She is sewing doll clothes, using her hands, loving her hands, loving them in the arduous business of manicures. The jealous mother's fingernails are pearls. Agnes wants to suck them. She wants to pet her mother's oily hair. She wants to ring a finger with it, play with its crimped, thick curliness. Netta's hair is black, too, nothing of Agnes's white blond is there.

And this is important: only Netta's hands are pretty, which is why Netta is so jealous of Agnes. Agnes is beautiful all over. That's the word used, *beautiful,* and once a boy in a boat used *radiant* to describe her. "The radiant Agnes under her umbrella," he said, then something else, but what it was Agnes does not remember.

Agnes does not want to remember everything.

Faye says that even parked near the glass doors, parked with no other place to look but out, our mother will not look out. She refuses to be jogged from the lake. Snowed-over shapes, rain, passing coats, none of what is happening around our mother is happening. The way our mother sees it, she is sixteen.

Agnes is sixteen years old. She wants to quit school, go to Italy, and study art. She is interested in the men, too, yes, sure, that's true. At sixteen, Agnes is a sweet sweet on sweets—she won't deny it. Also, and not to be forgotten, Agnes is rich.

No wonder then that Daddy wants her in the Shepherd, away from all the boys and to himself. No wonder then that she can't stay in school—could anyone? Agnes wants to go to Italy and paint, and oh—why not say it?—she wants to fuck around; she is luxurious.

Luxurious women do not need big breasts—that's a myth, although Agnes contends Daddy likes them. Lucky then that the witchy wife has them—and her hands, of course, her pearly nails; but Daddy likes his witchy wife's heavy breasts. These Agnes has seen Daddy straining after from as far away as the pier. They are a whiteness under the close lamp; the rest of Netta is smudged. Gray, beige, claret, brown, of these Netta usually wears brown. Even in the summer she wears long brown skirts and horrible

shoes, like men's shoes with stacked heels. The hats she
picks to wear are squat; flowers, birds, and clouds of veil
are perched on them. Each jewel she owns has a blouse
to go with it. Netta's is a grave style—but her daughter!
That Agnes! Her wispy daughter is another story. *Wispy,*
yes, *slight, whimsical, coy, feathered, birdlike, catlike* are all
words used to describe that girl.

Where did Agnes come from?

Who taught her how to dress?

Agnes is walking in mismatched shoes. She is wearing
white when she should not, wrong clothes to right affairs. To the parties her mother approves of, Agnes comes
breathless and late.

None of this matters now. Our mother can be late or she
can be early. "Calm down!" Faye says they have to say to
her. "Agnes, dear, calm down. You haven't missed a thing.
You're on time."

Our mother cries, "I am sorry," and she tells the nurses
that she is painfully, painfully, painfully shy, although no one
would know it to watch her. No one would guess how hard it
is for her to talk when there are so many people in the room.
Our mother is, she confesses, a long tremble. She stays in her
chair. She says, "I have to be careful I don't fall."

Our mother stays in her chair now most of the time, slack as a bathrobe, tottering, mumbling, giving her excuses to the floor.

"Yes," we say to Faye, "we have seen her, we can guess."

Our mother asks the same questions.

We are thousands of miles away from our mother—have been for years—and yet our mother asks, "Are you with Netta and Daddy? Are you out at the lake?"

Our mother says, "I don't think Netta likes me anymore. She never comes to visit."

That must be why Agnes goes back to the lake long after she has left sixteen: it is to see her witchy, jealous mother, who even from her bed on her back at eighty is castigating, "Agnes . . . what are we?" when Agnes is not sixteen anymore. She has not been any trouble for years, although she can't remember where she put her babies. Her babies, the boys, the dead ones—these are her troubles, these are what Agnes has to be sorry for.

There are dead horses in the home state, dead babies; she begins to make sense.

"Oh God, oh God, oh God, oh God!" our mother cries, or else Mother speaks to them, the boys, the dead babies. She says their names and cries.

Mother never says she drank.

Our mother has seen her sons through the scrim of the other side. She has talked to them. She tells Faye the boys are grown up. They are young men with Daddy's eyes.

"Not yours or yours," our mother says, and she swears at the nurses. "Yours are shit."

Faye tells us; Faye tells on Mother.

Faye says one of the nurses slapped our mother by accident when Mother tried to work her way out from under the belt they use to secure her. Our mother is a danger to herself and will sometimes try to walk. She will get to the lake however she can. "Better not try it!" Faye says, and she tells our mother it is cold outside. The lake is frozen.

Snowless, black, flecked with frosts, the lake is a starry sky with Agnes skating on it. She is a skater. No one would believe it to look at her—but look! Her ankles are bone; skates don't hurt. Only the cold hurts. It blows at the bridge of her nose and gives her a headache. Skating home, she is skating into the wind. The arctic air hits the tops of her legs, which is why she can't move them now! "For God's sake," Agnes says, "tell Netta to get the Epsom salts, and tell her no cold water, please!"

Our mother says the camp food stinks. She says, "Oh, boy, when I get home." When she gets home, she wants a lot of Hattie's custard. "Tell Netta," our mother has instructed us, my sister and me, "tell Netta to ask Hattie, please."

Faye says that the day nurses often report on our mother's unwillingness to eat. Our mother says, "This is not what I ordered!"

With Daddy it is baked Alaska. With Daddy it is the Waldorf, where Agnes wears a hat and lots of lipstick. The reason she has no eyebrows is she has no eyebrows! Her hair is still white blond but short, very short, a boy's on a face with a punched-out mouth. Some part of her there is always swollen. The ledge above her eye, a greater prominence in places prominent—here and here and here—Agnes tends these greater lumps. She wraps elbows in Ace bandages, holds ice against her jaw. "She is a mess," the witchy jealous mother tells anyone who asks. "What happened this time?" This time, like the last, Agnes simply did not look. She never looks but that she runs, runs after whatever it is rolling away on the incline. The witchy mother says, "Lucky Daddy isn't alive to see this."

Our mother's fingernails are yellow.

"Poor thing," Faye says, but she lets our mother ring and ring, knowing what it is she wants, which is just what she can't have.

❦

Our mother, on the phone, says, "My brothers don't like me. They think I am bad, but I am not. I am trying to be good. I want to go back to the lake." And she does.

Our mother is sixteen. Under the umbrella and oiled against the sun and half asleep, she is an open jam jar in the heat, a white honey, an edible fragrance, a light the boys look up at from their boats. "Agnes," they say, with nothing else to say. They use her name and idle near her, rocking on the wakes of other passing boys, always someone, someone waving, calling out, "Agnes!"

Agnes has a flask, too; Agnes drinks and smokes and knows the names to pills.

No wonder then that Daddy says, "In the boat, Agnes, now."

In the Shepherd Agnes holds out her hand and rakes the water. Agnes says, "Daddy is right about the boys. I always pick the wrong ones." Faceless men whose faces she knows are some of what she sees in the water.

Faye says our mother says that as soon as Daddy gets here, she is leaving. Cars can be heard cracking over the gravel. Our mother hears the cars and cries out, "Daddy's sent old Peter for me. I knew it!" The nurses wheel her out of the bingo room because she is crying. Our mother is crying,

"I want to go out in the Shepherd with Daddy and see the races."

Our mother, in her room, goes on and on about it, how she isn't good with numbers but she will try. She wants to play. Mother wants to go out again, please. She wants to try. "I'll be good, I'll be good, I'll be good. I want to get out of this shit-hole place. Jesus!" And his name, the way she says it, comes out sorrowful and red.

Then Agnes is not sixteen anymore but a woman with dead babies—only dead babies, which is surely what she means when she talks of the dead horses. Sets of silver and dishes, named cars, Italy long after she has thrown away her brushes, our mother does not ask anymore where it is packed.

A lot, of course, has been sold—had to be. Our mother's daddy is dead; the trust fund he left her is nearly depleted.

Our mother can't tell us apart on the phone, but she knows our voices. She remembers our names; and when we answer to them, she cries that she is ready. She wants to go back to the lake, to Netta, of course, and Daddy.

"Please," she says, "it's time."

Our mother's incessant cries, we can hear them when we are not on the phone. We can smell her when the nurses lift her into bed. We don't need Faye to tell us. We can see, we can see Agnes; she is a girl, and then for a long, long time she is not.

1960

Her arms belonged to a Hattie, potato-white, fat-puckered, floury-fat arms, which when she lifted them to put away the jam smelled sour. Hattie was a sour-smelling cook, finished work and in a coat—no sweater! Unbuckled boots and too-small scarf despite the cold. Outside in a running car Hattie's husband was waiting. He was the one to drive her. These were the baking days, those sighing days—less light and nearing holidays—when he brought Hattie here in the morning gloom and took her home, darkling.

Hard to see under the bill of his cap, a farmer's cap, and he, a farmer, smelling of mucked stalls and cheese. We had smelled him before. Mr. Rassmusen, Elmer Rassmusen as he was called by Netta, whose house it was where Hattie baked. "Mr. Rassmusen is here, Netta!" from us, waiting for the cookies to cool, the awful-sounding cookies that tasted so good: Springerle. "Does Mr. Rassmusen get any?"

Hattie says, "He has his heart to think about." Phony eggs and no bacon are what he has for breakfast now, poor man! They sold their chickens—what's the use? *Hardscrabble* is the word Frannie thinks of, and the cornstalks' yellow clatter in the wind when the wind blats through, as it mostly does, in our country in the dead of winter. What a phrase! Don't use it. The dead go nowhere; we have dug them up.

(Mother has some babies in the ground, but I think they do not sleep.)

Hattie says, "Be careful you don't burn your tongues," and she shuffles to the car in her unbuckled boots. The path is all ice and she is stooped against falling.

The thought of her bare arms beneath her rough coat makes us itch. Let's never be poor!

Poor Hattie was farm-poor and ugly, ugly and poor as the old women Netta visited. Netta took us to Miss Pearl's, whose cookies made us sick. "No thank you," we said, polite girls and sisters, born wide years apart but matching. Miss Pearl, the dressmaker, pinned us for approaching birthdays; but March was not as close as Netta thought. Uncertainties, instructions, moments of clarity and surprise, bright hurts.

(My mother's face in a mirror we once shared first informed me of beauty.)

Frannie is oldest; I am youngest. A sister in between would be nice—Frannie says. Frannie says it is sad about our brothers.

"Where were you girls?" from Netta, already thinking

of next year's Christmas, needling sequins to sew on a saddle. The camel is for the wise men on their journey. Across the desert! Under the stars!

Netta didn't know about the dog, how he plashed across the river and came home steaming. She didn't know how long we had played outside but that Hattie was here, yes; Netta said she could smell it, and we could, too: the onion odor of the woman mixed with butter and almond.

(Mother, I remember, unbuttoning even as she ran up the stairs, crying, "I can't stand myself!")

One day the pocky rain beat away the snow.

We made toffee without Hattie in the kitchen or Netta to boss us. The toffee was oversweet and hot and dripped off a stick—from the garden? Then our birthdays passed and we were *in* the garden. We were shoeless, sockless, and putting on a play that Frannie had directed because it was her idea in the first place.

Frannie's flaxen braids went past her waist so she could sit on them and play Rapunzel.

(Did I mention that our mother was an actress?)

Hattie was not a woman of expression or patience, but she played our audience and gruffed, "What girls you are! What made you think of this?"

Sometimes her surprise surprised us, as when we piled

what we picked out, which she then scolded us to eat. But who likes bitter rind in jelly? And why not swig vanilla? The way it smelled, we thought it would be sweet!

("She gets it from her mother," they say about me.)

Frannie is Frannie and *good, smart, responsible,* those stout terms grown-ups use on us wearing their accurate faces. Hattie does not have many faces. With her it's a scowl or a smile . . . and she looks like . . . Netta says, "Eleanor Roosevelt!" Hattie, apron off and in her everyday clothes, looks like Eleanor Roosevelt, top heavy, jowled, a preposterous hat. Her teeth, too—Hattie's—are made out of wood and wooden yellow.

Netta says to us, "Be thankful for what you've got."

"I am!" Frannie says, and I say, "We are!"

We are, we are, we are, we are everywhere running through the house, shooed out of rooms. "Go outside or watch TV!" In the old war footage the women wear scarves and rush across rubble.

"Aren't you glad you weren't born then?" Netta asks because she *was* alive then. She *lived* through the war although not as meanly; nevertheless, she says, "Really, aren't you glad you weren't born then?"

"We are!" but we like to pretend we are the dispossessed, and we pick at Hattie's coffee cake to make it last the war. The snow blows up and sideways, and what was close

outdoors is blurred in so much weather. Will Mr. Rassmusen drive through it? The whiteness squalls across the
fields.

(I miss my mother.)

Stranded in the country! Even the sander couldn't get
through to us, not to mention Mr. Rassmusen. Hattie said,
"His heart is old. . . . I hope he knows enough to stay at
home." By then the phones were down and the deep house
groaned. The sound was the sound of ice settling over the
lake, and we ran away from what we heard, ran throat-
hurt through our Netta's house. The magical house, the
big house, the house I wanted as my own. The doors when
opened huffed attic air, and we danced across the ballroom
and slid to the windows and saw snow-blind-close trees.
Who could get near us?

(In another house I put my mouth over Mother's and
cried down to a baby, "Can you hear me?")

Hattie is shouting into the dead phone so Mr. Rassmusen might hear. "See how the roads are tomorrow. Don't
drive!" This big, ugly woman is in tears. Thirty-five years
come June and she can count on her hand the nights apart
from Mr. Rassmusen. They met when they were not much
older than we are. Their daddies both farmed. But it's never

been dull, farm life. Farm life is full of incident: bladed equipment, animals, blood.

Tonight Hattie's story is the fox! Found midwinter, his flattened, frozen carcass breaks in half when P.J. bats with it. That P.J.! He came to collect Hattie once and walked in calling, "Ma!" There wasn't but the one car and Hattie beetling to it.

Out here the land is vacant. The fields look sad.

We should have a fire and sit close, knee to knee, feet to the flames—let the heat muddle us! We should get warm enough to wander. Netta's house is very large and unlived in without kids. Netta says she *loves* having us live here. "You have no idea," she says, "how much." We roam and look into and open; we make the house ours and use different tubs, strike fires in comfortable rooms, because Frannie can use matches. She lights the library fire and we sit with Hattie's cookies in our laps, eating, lazing, reading until we leave the stupefying fire to lean against the windows in the sunroom with the parrots. How cool it is, but what is that we smell? What is Hattie making?

Hattie says, "Now you're in the kitchen, do you want to help?"

We stand beating and beating the frosting, which catches on our arms, so we lick at ourselves until the frosting peaks and we can make a road down the middle. We're done! Done and dumbed with sugar and listening—*shhhhh*.

The plow makes cow noises as it lumbers up the hill, and somewhere men in clouds of snow are tossing sand and shoveling. Mr. Rassmusen, we hope, stays in; such strenuous work could kill him—his heart. His heart and his back! Hattie hopes the man is smart enough to make P.J. do it. P.J. is young. P.J. is not much older than we are; but he smells like a man to us, earthy and unsafe. Unshaved, unwashed, uncouth. *Uncouth?* Frannie's word. She can be a show-off, Frannie can. She can smarm her way into something sweet. Hattie simply forgets what time it is—almost dinner!—and she tells us stories. The day P.J. and his older brothers went shirtless near the forage blower and came out bloodied with their own blood or something else's. Hattie's stories. The sick-making smell of skunk and the mutt's whining home from it. Who dared go near him? Even when he smelled of himself or of the marshy water he swam in, that mutt was not a dog to get close to. The rats in her barn sleeked through the silage, fearless. Hattie's stories. Cows and horses, litters of kittens found egged in strawed places, this was how she lived. She left out sadness.

The coarse stink of onion grass and her rushed and dingy hairdo. Hattie in the sleeveless dress she wears to cook in—housecoat cotton, no matter the cold—Hattie is here when she is not here. Hattie's slippers and sleeveless dress she keeps in the backstairs bathroom. We have to hold our breath the whole time in there—hurry!

This happened in the middle of summer in the middle of another play of Frannie's devising. My part was small, but it called for me to swing the hammock until Frannie fell out. Of course, she fell too hard; but it was not, Netta assured me, my fault.

Hattie said, "It's both yews' fault."

I hated Hattie then.

Frannie had her cast signed so many times it looked like her yearbook page. Silly flowers and hearts in colored pens, accounts of love, old secrets. She wrapped her arm in plastic and held it in the air when she swam; she screamed if she thought I had splashed her. "Get a towel!" She was fearful the ink might run and the precious cast crumble.

(Mother used a hanger and scratched her own back bloody; I saw.)

Someone's coming; headlights rove over the snow, and Hattie hopes it is not who she thinks it is, but his headlights show in the falling. The rest is darkness.

(They say our mother is happier where she is.)

What did Hattie know then that we did not?

(Mother had her secrets; she had more than most.)

The passenger door was ledged with snow that sighed over Hattie when she closed it.

My dream began that all was blackness and terrible stars, yet they could see where they were going, and the roads, too, I thought, were cleared. They drove in heat and quiet, and Hattie took her scarf off and smoothed what she wore for hair. There wasn't much.

"Lick," Hattie saying. "Lick the spoon."

That smell I brushed against waiting at her waist for her lap.

Come back!

UNREDISCOVERED, UNRENAMEABLE

Before this, the island's outreachings—vetch, creeper,
bittersweet—the podded and nodding, all was bedlike
August and inviting us to sleep. But we didn't sleep; we
wanted to be self-sufficient and secure and scouted the
island to stockpile whatever could be eaten, burned.
Mother boiled rose hips and sweetened grains with berries
popped between her fingers—her slender fingers and their
used, bruised stains! Our mother, of course, knew how to
feed us; she knew which leaves to crush and hold against
our noses. Lemongrass, mint, lavender, thyme. With such
scents as these our mother soothed us, and at night she
told the stories with the cautions at the end: "That's how
accidents happen."

My sisters wanted to be the stories, central and adored,
but I was of an age that wanted stories about Father as I
was now, a boy whose swollen sex woke him with alarm,
and then the delight in its easing.

I wanted the story of Father's looking on, spellbound—
his word—by the simmering Oma stitching up her lip with
only whiskey to numb the work. Not that Oma drank
much. Not even her lip, split enough for stitches, could

make her drink. Nothing that happened to our father's mother's mother—not the lip, not the fire, not the loss of her Dora—could raw our Oma to tears.

Was I so brave as that? I didn't ask.

Our father's mother's mother was brave, and our father was brave, too. He was the one who cut down the suicide, that possum-ugly, mud-dark, urinous man. "Tell us again," but in the stories Mother repeated, our father came out married. He came out worn and running away, leaving Mother with the next bad job.

"Is that a true story?" we asked, unbelieving.

The island life was good then, but not so good as we would stay here.

Here, the ocean and its drama, an island cliffed and beaten by ferocious waves on one side and at the other flat and lapped. "Water, water everywhere and not a one of us can swim!" Our mother's song for us when Father took us to the pond. The pond, in the center of the island, was where we learned to swim, holding to the soft bank and kicking such a froth until the bridge of my nose burned from snorting water and it seemed I was water, blinded and blued with water, my face all snot and spit. "Let go!" Father said, and he kicked me loose, and I sank. This happened over and over again while Mother stood by singing.

*

Our mother says the mornings now are hardest and that I should know how many nights she cannot sleep unless she braces her body between the bodies of my sisters.

But I was speaking of before, before the rain washed out our start, our father, and the very boat that brought us; before the rain, the island was dewed and bejeweled with water caught in plattered leaves we drank from as from glasses. Deer, which must have clicked across the ice one winter, bounded past us, and there was smaller wildlife—fox, raccoon, rabbit, squirrel—and birds of northeastern, fall-serious colors. Mussels, periwinkles, dust-scuttling crabs, and bark-colored fish, the shallow water could be farmed, and we gathered what the high tide left behind. We gathered low-bush berries and mosses we could eat. This was our beginning, when the insistent squaw of seagulls crashing after urchins, susurrant grasses, and groggy frogs, the thin pitch, high pierce of insects was our music on any clear morning. The trees swept through the afternoon until stilled by the sun, they held themselves erect as candles, and the island flamed, and Father told my sisters, "Wish!" and they did, I think; I saw their mouths move. The island was in such ways silencing. The nights, guttering in kerosene, were starry and long—and the cold, the cold! Often I was witness to my mother when she held out her hands and said, "Look at how cracked," when she said, "No matter how beautiful it is here, I am lonely."

To me she confided how she missed seeing other people, simply people passing, strangers whose stories she liked to make up; and when she thought there was no one but us now to know her own story, she was sad.

I was a son. The island, I knew, would not always be my home—even if my sisters never married and pursued eccentric crafts, I would not come back to act as the stunted bachelor brother. My aim was to . . . well, I couldn't see an end exactly. The ordinary world we had left behind looked far away. The ordinary world from the island's highest point hung at a watery distance like laundry, like cold-smelling and sun-smelling coarse cloth. No harbor mess of lobster traps and low-tide stinks from here. From here, where I went sometimes for the view, I saw what we had left and what I could go back to.

Imagined blocks in fall's whetted light, fall's winds, a new smell, school.

But it was August. The island was hushed, and the pond where we swam was turned to scum. My sisters sulked. "Daddy," they said, "don't make us." I had no choice but to ease off the bank and into the water as example to my sisters, who yet resisted, saying, "He's a boy, Daddy, please don't make us."

The intoxicant of *swimming, swimming, swimming, swimming, swimming, swimming, swimming*! Alone, afar,

adrift from my family and Father shouting from the shore
made me wonder at the submerged and muffled experience
of water, which was also the experience of my age—four-
teen. I might sign on board if a boat passed near enough, I
might explore the mainland.

I saw my oldest sister's sex in sudden passing, a hairless
white hardness and a dark slot. I saw her and touched myself and was not ashamed. The island conspired to sex us;
the leaves, torn, milked, and there was hissing. The stones'
soft shapes marked and swashed by rising water—rising
water itself—ferns unfurling, teary gums and oozes from
the trees, slimes, foams, the sweat that fell from Mother's
face when she was bent to anything . . . all, all of it aroused
me. My sister, the oldest, yet not so old but that she wandered in undress, made me want to hurt her. What would
she feel like to squeeze?

The skin on her arm when I twisted it was hairless and
cool, and I could feel the bone in her arm, whereas the
youngest's arms were all flesh. The youngest was easier to
drag; her hip bones knocked against the stones; and she
bumped along the length I dragged her; yet she liked to be
dragged—they both did—and spooked and swung around
and chased and carried. Piggybacked and given up to jounc-
ing, the oldest sagged the reins by which she held me; and

she leaned back and looked up and in a clip-clopped voice noised her pleasure at the sky. So this was childish play, and I was aroused, and I kissed her.

She said, "What are you doing?"

"Act like someone else," I told her, and she didn't move when I touched her but stayed on her back and still.

The fog descended on the island, and the wind came up, and there was lightning where we lived. Our father died. Rain, rain, rain runneling down a mud slide, our father stuck and drowned. Mother made a spoon of her fingers and scooped mud from his eyes.

I begged against his ear to breathe.

My sisters cried.

On the cliff side of the island Mother beat me nearly deaf. "There are goats if that's your purpose," she shouted.

"But what is my purpose?" I asked, and I was mad in pain and sick and Mother said at first she didn't know what and then she did. "Why not stay here and people the island?" she asked. "Why not fuck me?"

WINTERREISE

Used to be even in the rain we walked hooded in water-repellent bicolor suits that swished and sounded as if we were fat when we were thin, both of us, Margaret and I, and only walking for the routine and the way it felt, hands free, holding nothing. Children, leashes—my first husband—we left even the dogs sleeping to meet each other at the entrance to the park marked by the great elm, that folktale tree with its house-wide trunk sprung green. We meet there still although not as often—and no more in the rain.

No more in the morning either, but in the afternoon when we are certain of the weather and the light, then we walk. We take the bridle path where the low, gnarled cherries cut the cutting wind off the reservoir. In spring the wind undoes the blossoms, and they snow on us; but in winter the stripped cherries are all black trunk and hugely tumored. Last winter Margaret asked that we avoid them, and we did. We took the road and went south beneath the sycamores. The sycamore, or plane tree, as my husband calls it, is a true city tree and seems always in autumnal leaf somehow, not yet exhausted, not yet stripped. Nothing, I think, not even the scarlet oak, Thoreau's favorite, can exceed the sycamore's assertive seriousness and grace, but my husband prefers the ginkgoes.

Margaret does not have a husband anymore to poll for his favorites—if he ever had favorites, trees that is, which I doubt. "A man," Thoreau says, "sees only what concerns him," and Margaret's husband has always been concerned with just himself. He does not write to or see his children. Not even when his grandson was born did the man think to call his daughter. His absence in the lives of his son and daughter has worried Margaret on our walks. She says, "I wish he would see them."

I start to say, but Margaret says, "I know what you're going to say—and thank you, really, I mean it."

We are in October, one of the great man's months, March being the other, and because I aspire to see as purely as Thoreau did, I read the essays at night and bring him with me on our walks. I like to think it cheers Margaret, and she says it does, although she says a lot of things, I think, to make me happy. Today, for example, when we meet at the elm, I see she stands unsteady in a wind that is quite gentle; yet when I ask her if she would rather not walk, she says, "No, no, no, I'm hoping to see something red. I'm ready."

There is little of red on our walks; the city mostly yellows. The ginkgoes are especially good at this. The fans that are their leaves never brown but turn, at the same instant, a like yellow. The trees look like matches, evenly planted, erect, and alight down the street. My husband admires them and is saddened, as am I, when the late rains thrash them from their branches.

But the ginkgoes have just begun to turn; we are not so far in the season, and Margaret and I have time, have weeks, I hope, to seek the reds, the sumac and the serviceberry, the flush of burning bush against the blue water when the water is blue and hard to look at in the afternoon angles of the sun. Near to the tennis courts and the north water station and the bridge this happens: the bridle path widens and rubbles and is hard to walk, so we turn onto the grassy swell and lean against the peeled trunk of a sycamore. We stop walking so that Margaret can catch her breath, and then it is we squint west, southwest across the water.

The reservoir wholly bright hurts memory enough to make a viewer weep, but Margaret—amazing woman that she is—doesn't. She looks at the water while I cry, not loudly, of course, not even a lot of sniffle, just the eyes wet but distorting and coloring the white water so that I don't see water but rather our collective past, Margaret's and mine; I see the afternoons we have spent together. Those days we shoved onto the rocky paths with our children strapped in strollers that sometimes stopped short with our cargo nearly thrown against the stones we would drive over. We bumped over curbs, too, recklessly, the way young wives do with their health so casually assumed, wagging bags of it shouldered loosely. In our neighborhood, Margaret's and mine, the bills fly for the simplest meals, although as young wives we made elaborate dinners, by the book, especially planned, costly. Parties these were, dinner parties for our young husbands and the other young husbands and wives from whom we hoped to gain—what?

So many of them now have left the city or moved to other parts of the city, met perhaps with their own disasters. I see few of the old gang anymore; only Margaret, really, from those times persists, lives, albeit alone, in the same prewar six in the Nineties off Fifth. If I press my cheek against her bedroom window, I can see the park.

Now when I visit her or when we walk, Margaret will remember someone we knew, and we will speculate about him and him and her. The couples—so many—what has become of? The little girls in French organza on the holidays—remember? The fabulous couple who sold apartments one after the other must have made a killing! Surely they are living grandly wherever it is in Connecticut. Margaret says, "I am not so sad they are gone."

"Me, too," I say, and we agree the quiet life now is what we wanted all along. We are glad the dinner parties are over, the silver wrapped and on the high shelf, the linens packed in tissues. No more the tedious procedures for making pies and peeling chestnuts; we have only to walk. Dinner will take care of itself; no one comes home hungry.

Margaret, especially, finds it hard to eat at night. Our walks are meant to help her appetite, but even the cannabis her son secrets her in hollowed books does not ease the way she has felt since—since when? I am not sure when. Margaret asked me to keep it a secret, and I did until a hot, dark night my husband came home and found me listening to Schubert's *Winterreise* and the last, most melancholy songs. He asked, "Is it so cold already?"

The *Winterreise* is music I save for January, which Thoreau found, as I do, the hardest month to get through. Winter, and the bridle path is impassable and even the road walked south is balked with ice and banked snow. When we walk in winter, we must walk slowly, although we walk very slowly all the time now.

The speed suits our purpose, although I must remind Margaret of this fact whenever she falls into a fit of apologizing, as she does often, saying, "I'm sorry, I'm sorry, I'm so slow." Then I remind her of what we are about on our walks. We are attending to nature. What business have I in the woods, Thoreau asks, if I am thinking of something out of the woods? So Margaret and I sit on the bench near the playground and look up at the honey locust's acid green. The underside of the tree is darkly branched, veined as a body is, a green heart. Everywhere, I find, the landscape gives us back ourselves, and when the etched bark of the suffering elm reminds me of my suffering friend who would keep, above all, her dignity, I weep. I weep, and I am out of the woods again!

Margaret says, "Don't you apologize now."

To live each day as well as we can was Thoreau's goal, and I want it to be mine—but to see my friend scarved like a pirate! Margaret's hair was once . . . it was once old yellows, greens, and blues. Schoolgirl thick, braided, bound, fantastically clipped in enormous clips, her hair was a feature untouched by her husband's leaving or the upset with her boy, his expensive confusions, his noisy failures. These disappointments had never disclosed themselves in Margaret's hair, although much of the rest of her contracted. Her brow was a scowl even sleeping. I knew. I had come upon her sleeping once and seen it: the arguments she must have had in sleep! This was when we drove to see her son at his college and slept in the last bed to be had in leaf season.

The leaves, I remember, and the colors on the toy-scale hills. Once we were beyond the broken and abandoned about the city—cones, netting, dividers, the many cautionary signs—the road widened and smoothed, and it seemed then we were alone and pioneering into the riotous crayoned woods of a time when teachers had said, "Color something special for Thanksgiving." Red, red, red, orange we admired all the way to the white and shuttered towns, the needle steeples of the churches and incorporated signs reading seventeen something, seventeen something, earlier and earlier all the way to Margaret's son, found lolling on a green once crossed by minutemen. "Imagine!" we had extolled, though nothing impressed him.

The boy had said, "I'm not getting anything out of school, Mom. I want to take a year off instead. I want to travel."

Margaret said, "Peter"—his name—"Peter, will you use your head!"

The boy stayed on another year writing lackluster papers on the history of art, then groaning home for holidays—another Christmas, another Easter. He blued the apartment with French cigarettes until his weary mother said, "So travel, if this is what you want." The boy worked his way across—across oceans, continents, misogynistic countries—forgetting what he looked like in the dirt-poor towns, the kind he was after. He wrote, "I've had enough of comfort," so that who would have guessed his unexpected self-discovery? Cabinetmaking! Which he practices with mixed results near what was once his college.

Margaret, on our walks, sometimes speaks of him, of Peter, she begins, "If I had—"

Thoreau would have us live with nature in the present, above time.

But it is hard to live above time. The church bell sounds the hours and the neighborhood streets are trafficked with our pasts, backpacked students in a jangle of keys, fretful mothers. Weekday mornings, afternoons, the coffee shops clog while kids pool change. Must be three-thirty, school out, nearing four, I guess, until the ambulance's wail or the pushy must of fire trucks, the clamor of it all, insists it is ongoing and anytime; this is a city.

This is a city, but we are in the park. We are straining to be in the park, Margaret and I, and out of reach of time and memory and sickness, which yet wash back beneath the trees. Nothing withstands sensation; the tremulous body will not hold still or still enough in the present to catch, by hand, small fish. But Thoreau, Thoreau could hold himself so stilly that rodents burrowed in his pocket, snakes slithered at his feet. He stood, as any tree might, ready, alert, large; the scrambling world would nest in him, he was in such ways constant and outstretched.

I am not so generous.

Once invited to hold her in bed, I took up Margaret's hand instead and petted it, and when the nurse came in with her cruel means to relief—sharp objects, colorless drugs—I said, "I'll just step out for a bit."

The soldierly Thoreau drums past me; I am not brave. The slick at Margaret's neck I know for sweat I will not touch for fear of catching what she has, and this is stupid, I know. I am ashamed of these feelings and of much else that I imagine when we are walking: the sea's disgorged of ship-wreck on Cohasset's rocky shore. I see what Thoreau saw of the brig on Grampus Rock. The matted, livid, swollen, and mangled, his adjectives, piled easily as salvage, yet he would look at the dead as at a gown or scarf or tossed-up bon-net. Such losses in indifferent winds are sung, yet he would look, Thoreau, he had his pencil, surely, his diary.

Margaret has said, "I would like you to help me pick out a dress. I want pearls around my neck for the viewing.

"I want to look at the Great Thing boldly," she says.

I want to look at trees and not at losses past or those to come; yet the boles in the trees, those trees struck half dead, the startled quality of the exposed and leafless, the dusty feather-duster grasses waving in the shallows their piteous good-byes—oh, the undulant lot of it moves with meaning! Nothing is only what it is, but we must—I must—insist on its underside, its theme, when what I have on my arm is just my friend.

My friend is fifty-six years old; the female parts of her have been scraped out. Her face is plucked, sketched. The enormous forehead is an oiled stone; the balled lids are lashless. Whatever came before and marked her has been sanded away.

The husband who left her on the side of the road—gone.

Gone the restless son, the sometimes sickly daughter.

Betrayals, losses, the inane nights alone slip like shawls from off her shoulders, lightly, and the late light turns her gold.

She says, "The clarity of it all"; she says, "My heart." She is elusive, of course; she is dying. Thoreau, on the morning of his death and being read to, is said to have said, "Now comes good sailing." Quotable to the very end, he is a hard, clean object, a white stone in dark water, woods, greens, needles underfoot. He is a walker; he walks a distance, as we would, from here to here.

THE BLOOD JET

Neck pricklers, irritants, the papery labels seemed glued on, and I cut them off before I wore the shirts he gave me for no reason and which for no reason he often threw away. He was the boss, of course; he could do what he wanted. He insisted we visit the murdered wife's house, where, poking and poking with his finger at my head, he said, "Bang, bang, bang," then told me how the banker husband shot her. He took me backstage to meet famous musicians. Rich friends he knew gave us tours of their estates, and he hinted at his own wealth's growing. He showed off his full-deck-thick clipped wad of money and the diamond his mother once wore on her hand. "It could be yours," he said, "if you behave."

What a life this was!

He picked limes over lemons every time, and he liked toothpicked onions in his dry martinis. Martinis and daiquiris and old-fashioneds, scotch on the rocks, margaritas with salt. He was a drinker; this was in the eighties. I was thirty-six or thirty-seven but in surprising ways quite young.

Imagine growing up outside a village with one of everything, a dress shop, a dealership, a river. Everything named for what it was—so many Nancys and Barbaras and Judys, and most in passed-down clothes that must have itched.

I, I was skin sensitive even then.

He said, "You think you're so much better than me."

"No," I said, "I don't," and though I lied—and did think he was coarsely born—he was lying, too, when he made up his moneyed past and passed off the powerful as friends. They were simply his clients, and he was treating. And there never was a second wife, adored, a well-born blond named Amy. She was nowhere in his apartment; I looked. The dispossessed stood landlocked and small in his famished pile of photographs: fences, stoops, indoor fights, and no sign of Amy at all. His apartment had an overwarm, shut-in smell—too much man! Black hand towels, beige furniture, space-age lamps with saucered hoods, and sharp-edged ashtrays, surely gifts. The bookends were fashioned from golf clubs, and the books were, most of them, thrillers. No pictures of the living anywhere, not even of his daughter, the one he talked of, saying, "You don't look like her. She's pretty."

How can I explain what I did next? I let him move in and forgot my daughters and made myself presentable. This involved shopping and spending his money or returning what he had bought me. I returned two expensive dresses, kept the watch and ruby earrings (rubies!), exchanged the scratchy mohair sweater and the clothes with chains for decoration, the frilly perfumes. He had someone else in mind, or he pretended there was someone else, and often when we fucked, he called me Amy.

I called him nothing; he was as he was. His torso was creased from the folds of his bellies, and his unmuscled legs rasped walking. He moved slowly yet sweated; even newly ironed, the armpits of his shirts smelled sharply, and the strained seams of his worn pants advertised his ass, his hairy ass now in heavy motion, thrusting. I was dumbed to saying nothing, to calling him nothing but a cock, a very big cock. What else could you call that red trumpeting thing he slapped across my face?

My skill was spending, he said, and I sure knew how to do it. He said, "Where's your wallet, cunt?" when we both knew where it was, at home, on my dresser, empty. He said and he said, "No one cares about you. You think you're pretty? Look again." Foam flecked the corners of his mouth when he spoke; his lips were fat. He drank. He said my husband was smart to trade me in and only he was so dumb as to stay on—oh! Oh, it pissed him off, seeing me, and I was greeted with presents he tossed in gritted rage. My friends wondered why I put up with it. I said, "I think I must hate my life—I must." I did!

Even on the island, where the tree frogs chirruped tunefully, I thought about other islands I had been on, and I spoke my husband's name out loud and sentimentally. I indulged in feeling sad; I said, "I can't help myself" too many times until the long long-distance calls I made home angered him to whining on the phone, "Babies, I miss you, I do." He imitated me in a hideous voice, or else he shouted, "Why don't you ever look at anything? Why don't you see what there is to see?"

He was right, of course. I thought of the past; I compared. I considered skin—was it porous or not? Don't ask me to describe his. I will tell you that he had slightly feminine highbrow taste. His shirts, for instance, were French cuffed and very soft. So why didn't he think soft with me?

He was never nice, yet I let him move in. This, I thought, was experience. This was preparation for some life or this was life after a certain age: acutely felt, clearly flat. No romance.

My daughters hated him. The oldest said she would never come home. "I'll stay at Gran's," she said, "and so will Cissy," although he liked Cissy, so I sometimes arranged to get Cissy, and we went out together, the three of us. Once we went to a soda shop, and he ordered a sundae—a sundae!—he spooning off and feeding her the whip cream. Prissy, he called her, also Little Dope, Cis Miss, Stupid Puss, Sis. At least I never let him drive Cissy anywhere—I was that much a mother—yet I, who was meant to look out for the child, I drove too fast and drunkenly when I took Cissy back to her gran's, my mother's, that bitch's.

Crying then, always crying, I called Cissy my baby. She was my baby, my youngest and favorite. Cissy, my favorite, turned forward, hair beaten back, the curls on her baby head whapped straw dry and stiff by the time we got there—"Home again, home again, jiggity jog"—singing all the way to Mother's house, where my oldest daughter was somewhere inside and would not see me. Even my mother stayed behind the screen when she spoke. Mother was afraid of me, I think, when I was the one without children, outside. Because of him, I think, I lost them. I blamed him and I blamed my ex-husband, blamed my mother, everyone. . . .

"Why did you let him into your house?" my mother said.

Why did I?

He pulled the plugs to lamps to turn them off. He took pictures from the walls and broke them. I was afraid of what he would do. He poked with a hanger after tags I might have buried under rinds and smearing grease. The whiskey sediment in last night's glasses, last night's bloody plates. Violence and sickness. The dried-out, board-hard dish towel in its contorted, twisted shape. All was fragmented, unfinished, discomposed. "Why don't you get a fur coat?" he asked. "Call your friend what's-it's. She'll know"—*unlike you* the unspoken parenthetical at the end of whatever he said to me. Easily cruel, the man scissored stitches to the large griefs and the small griefs, his expression seeming mean or sad.

I began to think he was lying about his daughter, the pretty girl who never came to see him; and he was hateful to the boy who called some evenings asking for his dad. "Don't call me here again," he said to the boy. "You little fuck, it's none of your business."

The times I cautioned him, "Remember, he's your son," he said, "What do you know about being a parent?"

What did I? My oldest daughter vowed never to visit.

My oldest daughter said, "You hate everyone," and she was right: I did hate many people. I hated disproportionately, vociferously, indulged in wrathful scratching and saying how I hated . . . I hated my mother, my ex-husband, him. Any inconvenience—"We don't have," "We won't take," "We can't do"—abraded old sores or made them, and I berated and insulted and slurred helpless persons and said *fuck* and *fucking* all the time. My daughters, witnessing, trailed with puzzled faces. "Will you fuck off?" I said to them—and to him.

I especially hated him and thought, If I only had his money. . . . For he had money, and money gentles everything, except when it is given cruelly; then the thwart of cancellations and delays abrades. Think of a starchy collar against a sunburned neck.

ℐℨ

A day in spring too bald yet still pastel, the wind is hard through the trees. We are touring the murdered wife's house, where the carpeting sweeps through the gaping rooms—few divisions, recessed lights, marble surfaces, money. The banker husband's, surely; what is she but aggravation—a threatening debt, stupidly indifferent. "A bit like you," the man says to me, "a lot like you." He says, "So go on. So *waah, waah, waah* about money," but his hands come first.

I am saying horrible things and hitting back, and we are standing in the murdered woman's bedroom. The house belongs to no one now until the bullet holes are fixed and someone else wants to live here. We don't!

I already owned a house, but in the summer, for my sake, he rented within walking distance of the beach. The season cost as much as a car, but the house on the lane was invisibled by hedges, and I had lots of time on my own there—no children. So what did I have to complain of? That's what he wanted to know.

At night, weepy, I wandered out of doors to such sensations as I had had once with a boy who fanned his hair for me to sleep on—soft.

The heat blows through the summer rental; the house billows or seems to, and I am glad glad glad the man is gone!

I can call my girls now and talk and talk until my tongue swells, and I am tired.

Cissy on the phone scolds, "It's always sex with you, Mother. I'm too young."

I was thirty-six, yes, thirty-six, and he was older by eleven years exactly. He said he would die first, especially with me around, but he promised trust funds for the girls, so I stuck it out carelessly and heard time clang past.

Why didn't I have more fun?

Once, in the beginning, before the neighbors, before the cops, he met us at the zoo. Cissy, I think, suspected he was coming, or something like him, something large and wheezing and hairy. Cissy, as a child, was open arms to anybody, but when he made to speak, she cried for me to lift her.

Why didn't I take my child to me and run?

He said from the start he was a misanthrope, but I didn't believe him. I thought . . . I thought adult life was meant to be uncomfortable, full of anguish and embarrassment; but after a while, I felt no embarrassment. What people saw, they saw.

The real estate agent saw us rushing from the murder scene to the lawn, saw this fat man hitting me, and me hitting this fat man, and both of us screaming how we hated and swearing we would—yes, definitely, today, no more fucking around but seriously over now, no more, before we killed each other.

Think of poisonous solvents that smoke through cloth. Think of miseries, stinks. He was steak-red and fat, and we were both full of wine when the house winked in high sun, a bloody charge against my eyes.

"Some renovation," the real estate agent had said, and it could be ours.

No thanks! I wanted to live at home again with my mother and the girls, but I didn't know how to ask.

"What a fucking sad sack!" he said. He said horrible things, but I said worse.

The real estate agent in her locked car leaned on her horn as if, like water on the rabid, it would startle us apart. The dusty snarl of us, us on the front lawn in full sun fighting. Sun! How I cursed it! Heat chafed, itchy, cankered, and confused by the freakish rush of summer, and this man pushing me against the car, saying, "Get in, goddammit, before I kill you."

Do it! Do it! Do it! was my heart—is still my heart when I think of him, and I think of him. I wonder at that tin-bright vision, that acidic bite of spit, that embrace, that poetry by which I live.

About the Author

Christine Schutt is the author of the short-story collection *Nightwork* and the novel *Florida,* a finalist for the National Book Award. Her work, which has garnered an O. Henry Prize and a Pushcart Prize, is published widely in literary journals. Schutt lives and teaches in New York City.